FUELED BY DRAGON'S FIRE

RETURN OF THE DRAGONBORN BOOK 2

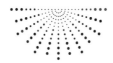

N.M. HOWELL

Written in collaboration with

H.F. STARK

Cover by

COVERS BY JUAN

DUNGEON MEDIA CORP.

PROLOGUE

THE DRAGONS HAVE RETURNED.

It began as a rumor. A rumor like any of the hundred others that had been spread countless times over the centuries. But not once had they proved to be anything other than fabricated stories. Lies propagated by governments and institutions to incite fear and chaos throughout the great land of Shaeyara. Such a rumor had spread so frequently that this time no one seemed to care.

No one even blinked.

It had already been some time since the University in Arvall was ruined and shut down, but still, no one fully understood what took place there that night. No sense could be made from that wreckage. All the world knew was that the University had finally been toppled from its pedestal. The inhabitants of Arvall, one of the greatest cities of all of Noelle, all believed the professors to have gone crazy. As, after all, no one living had ever seen a dragon. Those creatures and their masters had not walked the earth in centuries, and it was insane, impossible even, that they had returned. No one believed it.

Not until they saw for themselves.

The dragons and their riders were first seen in the skies over Abhainn. Even from a thousand feet below, the dragons seemed like enormous manifestations of nightmares. People ran screaming, gathering their children and searching for shelter. No one had ever seen such creatures, such magnificent and terrible beasts that could cut the sky with speed like a thousand celestial knives. They had all heard the stories. Dragons were vicious beasts, capable of slaughtering villages in minutes with their fire. Dragons were evil beasts.

Or so the people were led to believe.

From the moment the first dragon was seen in the skies, rumors spread like wildfire through a brown field, to even the farthest reaches of Noelle. Even to the mine cities in the north where hardly any news ever came or went. Rage and panic began to move through the people. Several attempts were made to find the dragonborn, but it was impossible to track them. The dragons were too fast, and when they sensed they were watched, they could soar so high the eye could not follow them through the clouds.

When the tales began spreading from all corners of the land, however, people began to believe. What everyone once knew to be outlandish stories had finally come alive. The rumors spread by those who survived that horrible night at the University were finally believed. Not only did this mean the dragons had returned, but it also confirmed the deaths of all eight-hundred innocent people who had lost their lives in the mirror hall of the University on the night of their return.

The dragons killed them, people claimed. The evil dragonborn warriors brutally attacked the University that night, a great and angry race who had no business existing in modern time.

Fear grew among the people of Noelle, and the University was only spoken of in whispers for fear of drawing the dragons near. Although many were glad to finally see the University deposed as the leading influencer of Noelle, the people who died were most of the over one-thousand diplomats who had traveled to Arvall to enjoy the Winter Festival. The abrupt and terrible end of so many world leaders left Noelle in utter, devastating confusion as hundreds of politicians across the country clambered over each other to fill the power vacuum. Each claimed to be the one strong enough to lead the people to victory against the evil dragonborn and their dragons. The world waged war.

The threat of the dragons and their riders loomed over the land, increasing with each day that passed without the dragons being found. And so, all the world lived in fear.

But there was at least one who knew the truth.

CHAPTER ONE

ANDIE STARED DOWN INTO THE ENDLESS DEPTHS OF the chasm that spread across the largest cavern they'd come across yet. Her toes clung dangerously over the edge, and the cool, damp air sent goosebumps up her arms as a strange breeze made its way up from the abyss, the wind a haunting song in her ear. "There's no way out," she whispered.

Their party had traveled through nearly every tunnel and corridor in their search for a way out, but they just kept going in circles. Every path eventually led back to that same cavern with the chasm they could never hope to cross. She was tired, hungry, and had grown thin and pale in the near constant darkness they had been living in for the past few months. Worse still, she had ceased to feel the connection to her people and their magic.

She feared for herself and her friends, but she worried more for the dragonborn out there in a modern world that wanted them slaughtered. A world that must be completely foreign and unwelcoming to them, and so far from home. She knew that with her and her friends trapped underground, nothing but evil rumors would spread throughout Noelle. Whether the University had shut down after their bloody battle or not, she knew in her heart they wouldn't stop until her people were found. Until her people were destroyed.

"Ow."

Carmen's voice pulled her out of her reverie. She had broken her ankle weeks before, and without their magic, they hadn't been able to mend it. Andie went over to her and kneeled beside her and began to rewrap the torn shirt tied around Carmen's ankle. It needed to be tighter. Even after all the time that had passed, her ankle still hadn't healed. Andie thought it was finally better some weeks ago, but when they found the bone was mending at the wrong angle, Marvo had to rebreak it. That certainly hadn't been their best night.

All of Andie's injuries had healed because of her dragonblood, but Carmen couldn't heal herself without a spell, which would bring the Searchers right to them. Since the night of the battle in the archives, the University had been monitoring the icons that remained implanted in Andie, Carmen, and Yara's hands. If any of the girls so much as cast a simple levitation spell, the University would know exactly where to find them. That was not an option. Not after all the trouble they had taken to hide themselves where no one would think to look for them.

"I'm so sorry, Carmen," Andie said as she yanked the wrapping as tight as she could. "I never meant to get you in this mess. I never meant to get any of you in—"

"I'm old enough to make my own decisions," Carmen snapped, ever defiant. "I did what I needed to do to protect my friend, and I would do it again. We'll get out of here, Andie, and we'll win. We'll win."

"Yeah." Andie wasn't so sure. Their party grew weak, and their chances of survival decreased with every passing moment.

"You know, this isn't the first time I've had to look out for one of my friends." Carmen unsteadily pushed herself to her feet and began collecting whatever small sticks and withered vegetation she could get her hands on to make a fire. "Raesh doesn't talk about it, but something happened when we were younger. I don't know if he ever got over it. Did he ever tell you?"

Andie took the sticks from Carmen's arms and began making a small fire away from the edge of the cavern. It took her numerous tries with the limited supplies they had collected, but eventually, the flame took and cast a much-needed warmth over their shaking bodies. Carmen curled on her side next to the fire, and Andie joined her, eager to hear what she had to say.

"When we were eight our parents took us to Taline. We were going to stay in a hotel there for a little while. It was back when they still had the Glass Games. You probably don't remember it, but there was loveglass everywhere in the most beautiful and brilliant shapes. The athletes were so talented; I remember one of them offered to take me on a short run and my parents said yes. He took me all the way up to the thirteenth floor of a building, then we swirled and flipped and drifted back down. It was incredible. Raesh was scared to be in the city then. I guess all the people and the size of the buildings scared him. I held his hand as we walked through the city."

Andie did remember. She held her hands out in front of the small fire for warmth as she listened intently to Carmen's story. She had never heard this story before. Obviously, it was one Raesh didn't want her to hear, or else he would have told it to her himself. Nevertheless, she listened quietly as Carmen reminisced, staring dazed out into the dark corners of the cavern.

"Anyway, we'd been in Taline for a couple of nights already, and then one day we were around midtown, just looking for new collar robes for my father. I looked up, and I saw this pair of Red Ravens flying in circles above us. They say it's a sign of great fortune to have the ravens dance over you, to be chosen by them." A flash of a smile crossed Carmen's lips in the flickering firelight, but the smile was quickly replaced with a haunted expression. "I was so excited. I grabbed Raesh and pointed to the sky. But when I looked up again, the ravens had changed color and were flying away. I never knew until then that they turn black when they're scared. But I looked down Owl's Line, the main boulevard of the city, and there was this huge purple wave crashing toward us. By the time we knew what it was, the explosion had already reached us. Every one of us was knocked off our feet. I can't even describe what it was like. Hot, powerful, relentless energy. I've never seen anything like it. I can still hear the screams."

Andie nodded solemnly along to Carmen's recount. She knew it well. "The first terrorist attack in Taline. They've been plagued by them ever since."

"When the blast wall passed us, I couldn't find my parents or Raesh's. The air was so thick with dust. My eyes were burning, and my ears were ringing. A few moments passed, and I realized I could hear Raesh. He was screaming. He'd gotten thrown through the glass window of a nearby store, and his legs were buried in debris. But the building was collapsing; the debris was already falling off of it as the building collapsed in on itself. But I couldn't leave him there." A single tear trickled down Carmen's cheek. Andie pretended to look away as she wiped the evidence away with a torn sleeve.

"What happened?" Andie asked.

"I ran inside, ducking through the people rushing out. I helped him dig himself out, and then I half carried him out. I barely got him out in time before the entire building had collapsed right where he had been trapped. Our parents found us, took us up, and ran. I almost lost everyone I loved that day."

"You saved Raesh," Andie said, her eyes tearing lightly. "That's an incredible story. Is that why you're so… so…"

"Headstrong?"

"I was going to say protective."

Carmine laughed. "Yeah, that works, too. It's strange. That day helped make me who I am, but what I remember most isn't the explosion or the chaos. It's all those people running out of that building and ignoring that little boy stuck in the debris, screaming for someone, anyone to help him. To save him. I could never understand how people could be so cruel and so selfish."

"Fear and the unknown can make a person do anything, but more often than not it just shows you who you really are." These words held more meaning to Andie than Carmen could ever know. "But you didn't run. You saved him. You're a hero."

"No. I'm just someone who won't leave a friend behind. Where were you that day?"

"I was at home," Andie said, trying to hold onto her emotion. She turned away from Carmen and looked back to the chasm behind them. "I never saw the explosion."

"You're lucky."

Andie nodded. "I…" she began, but she couldn't bring herself to say the words. The memories of that day have haunted her since she was a child. It was the day her mother had been taken away from her. The day her mother had been killed.

Andie managed to hold herself together with the exception of a few tears that refused to obey her. She turned back to Carmen and offered the most genuine smile she could. Carmen reached out to wipe Andie's cheek with her own sleeve and took hold of her shaking hand. She gave Andie a moment to breathe, to calm. They had gotten to know each other enough over the past few years that Carmen knew there was more going on behind Andie's eyes than she let on.

"Andie, I'm so sorry. I didn't mean to bring up anything painful for you."

Andie shook her head, and a hoarse laugh sounded from her throat. "No, no. It's fine. I'm fine."

"I only mentioned the story so that you know

beyond the shadow of a doubt that I will never abandon you. Whether it's a falling building or racist professors. I'll be here."

Carmen took Andie's other hand and gave it a light squeeze. Andie could tell from her hands just how weak her friend had gotten. Carmen yawned, and Andie pulled her pack over for her to use as a pillow while she rested. Andie offered a final smile and got up to go back to the precipice, leaving Carmen to rest. There was something about staring into that cold and endless void that took Andie's mind off all the problems waiting above ground. She glanced back momentarily to Carmen, who had already fallen asleep next to the dying fire.

After what seemed like an endless amount of time trapped in her own thoughts, Raesh walked up beside her and stood silently. He did that often, always knowing when to speak and when to be silent, almost as if he were reading her mind. He knew her that well. Right then Andie was hoping that he knew what she needed, which was to hear his voice, even if it was only bad news. She had grown to love that voice over the past few months, not that she would ever admit that to him. Not after she had brushed him off for so long while she was at the University. It was just one of the many things she regretted.

"Eight months," he finally said to her. "That's how long we've been stuck down here, roving back and forth through these tunnels, looking for a path that isn't here."

"What else can we do?" Andie asked, still staring out into the black. "It's almost a hundred percent guarantee at this point that there's only one way out of this place, and it's probably guarded with hundreds of professors. Without the dragonborn here to back us up, we'll never make it out alive."

"We have the dragonborn," he said. "We've got you."

Andie stood silent for a long moment. "I'm not enough."

Raesh turned to her, slowly, deliberately. For a moment, he just stared at her, as if he couldn't believe the words that had just come out of her mouth. "I don't ever want to hear you say that again. You're all we'll ever need."

She shared a look with him then that escaped her ability to define. With the immensity of the pressure and the reality of their situation, there hadn't been much time for romance, but she felt it whether he was near her or not. And she knew he felt it, too. It just wasn't the right time to act on it.

"Raesh," she began. "It's just that now...we can't really...I know what I've put you through with Tarven and the Archives and...the timing—"

"Isn't right," he said, nodding. "I know. Maybe someday."

13

He smiled at her and then left. She felt incredibly grateful. She turned around, looking for Marvo, and couldn't help but smile at Carmen snoring softly on the ground, curled up next to the burnt-out fire. Yara was also asleep, sprawled out near the dregs of the food reserves. They hadn't been able to scavenge in a while, and their reserves has gotten dangerously low. Andie's stomach grumbled just thinking about food.

She wrapped her arms tight around her waist, hoping no one had heard.

CHAPTER TWO

Marvo's fighters were scattered over the tunnel, sleeping, staring, eating, or finding some small way to pass the time, which was all they'd really had since the group came into the tunnels. Marvo was walking toward her, picking his way through the seated bodies and trying to dole out smiles as he went. He reached her undaunted, even though only one person had smiled back at him.

"It's getting harder to keep everyone motivated, Andie," he said. "A lot of them have already given up, and every day we lose a few more to this depression. We're dying down here. I think it's pretty clear now that the only way out is the way we came."

Andie stared at him with wide eyes, but in her heart, she knew what he said was true. "If we go back the way we came, they'll slaughter us for sure."

Marvo nodded. "I agree, but if we're just going to die down here anyway, it's a risk we need to take. If we'd known this eight months ago, we'd have had no problem fighting our way out, but we're weak now."

"I know. Even with my own healing abilities, I'm finding myself growing weaker by the day. But if we try to face what's up there, I don't think we'll win."

"We'd have to approach it cleverly. We do have the element of surprise. They don't even know we're down here."

"We hope they don't. But even if we surprise them, we don't know what we'd be walking into. There could be no one up there, or there could be hundreds. We chose to come here to the tunnels under the University because we thought it was the last place they'd look for us, but that whole plan was contingent on them not knowing we're down here. If they've figured it out, they could just be waiting."

"We sent up scouts," Marvo said, his hands on his hips. "They just got back an hour ago."

"What?" Andie asked, excited and anxious at once. "Any good news? What did they see?"

"Nothing, but they only went as far as the cafeteria to scavenge some more food. They didn't see anyone at all, and they didn't hear anything, but that's not conclusive."

"It could be a ruse," she said, deep in thought.

"Make the scouts think everything is okay so that we all go up."

"Possibly. But we can't continue like this. We need to get above ground. We might have won the first battle, but you know that this is far from over. The University has been in power for hundreds of years, and there is no way they're going to just give that up. If by some chance they go down, they'll do their best to bring the whole world with them." Marvo ran his hands through his hair as he spoke, his eyes narrowed in intense desperation.

"I agree."

"You know as well as I do that the lies about your people and their dragons have probably already spread coast to coast. Chancellor Mharú looked like a man on a mission, and he's had eight months to get his poison into Noelle. Factor in the droves of professors who are just as angry and hateful as he is, and you can imagine what that many powerful sorcerers can do."

Andie turned away from him, contemplating. Her mind was racing for a solution, anything that would help her escape having to risk the lives of everyone again. There had been so much death that night. She couldn't handle anymore. She wished she could find the connection to her people. She knew they would know what to do or even be able to rescue them. But the dragonborn had their own problems, and she and the rest of her party underground were alone.

17

"Maybe I can make it to the other side of the cavern," she said. "I think I could still be strong enough. We don't know what's on the other side. It could be our salvation."

"Andie, you're not listening," Marvo said, gently but firmly taking her by the shoulders. "We have to get out of here. And there is only one way to do that. You know it."

Andie looked at him, wanting to disagree, to fight him on it, to save her friends. But she knew he wanted to spare them as much as she did. And she knew he was right about what they had to do. She could see his heart breaking in his eyes. And then it hit her, solidly and without any illusions. The war for the heart of Noelle had only just begun.

"Okay," she said with a deep breath. "We'll all come together, finish the rations, and then leave as soon as everyone's rested."

Marvo nodded in response and then turned to go. He took a few slow steps away and then turned back to Andie, his expression softened into one of compassion. "Hope is not lost, Andie. We still have a chance at survival."

Marvo's words filled Andie with a flicker of hope, but she dared not hold onto it for risk of setting herself up for disappointment. She knew their chances of survival were slim to none, but she supposed she could offer him what little faith she had left. When

Andie finally nodded in agreement, Marvo turned again and left her to her own thoughts.

Andie spent a few more moments at the precipice before she came down to be with her friends. Scenarios of their escape ran rampant through her mind, none of which featured a desirable outcome. Still, she trusted Marvo's instincts. If he truly believed they had a chance, she would do everything in her power to make sure it happened. Andie closed her eyes and let out a deep breath she had been holding, the cool breeze that blew up from the depths of the chasm offered her a moment of peace. Finally, she opened her eyes and turned to gaze out at those who remained of their party.

Raesh was over with Kristole, talking something over vehemently. Carmen had begun stirring, possibly from a bad dream or the pain in her ankle. Yara was waking up, and she smiled when she and Andie made eye contact. Yara beckoned her over, and Andie went to join her friend. She and Yara had grown close over the past eight months. They had been friends at the University too, for sure. But something changed when they embarked on their journey underground. The two had grown closer than sisters, and Andie always relished the moments they shared together, no matter how brief.

Yara offered Andie one of the last pieces of stale bread from their stores, but Andie refused as she sat down next to her friend. Yara shrugged and nibbled on the bread, and from the expression on her face, Andie imagined it hadn't kept all that well in the damp cavern. The two chatted quietly between themselves for some time, about nothing and everything all at once. They strengthened each other while Andie told Yara about the new plan. Yara seemed as uneasy about it as Andie was, but she knew what needed to be done. Perhaps that was why Andie had grown so close to her. She was always the first to act when anything was needed, and she supported Andie in all her decisions. She was the rock that grounded her.

Not too long later, Marvo made the announcement to everyone. There wasn't much of a reaction from the fighters. Like Marvo had said, they seemed to have given up completely. Raesh did what he could to rally them, but they mostly just sat down to eat and then drifted off at their own paces. Hardly anyone seemed to even listen or care. They were defeated, and Andie's flicker of faith began to go out as she looked on at the faces of the men and women around her.

"I know what this looks like," Marvo said loudly when it became clear his troops weren't responding to his announcement. "It must seem like suicide. Like we fought all those people and sat through all those nights of planning just to die here, in the dark. But that's exactly what we're trying to avoid. We can't stay here anymore, not if we ever want to see our families again. There is no way out of here, no back way, no secret passage, no magical tunnel waiting to be revealed."

Marvo's fighters began to stir. Andie listened from a distance with a small smile on her face. She was the reason they were all down there, and it was her duty to lead them to safety. But these were Marvo's men, and she knew only he could be the one to truly convince them of their strength.

"The only way out is back where we came in, and we all know what is waiting there," Marvo continued. "But I'm not scared. How can I be? We beat them once, and we'll do it again if necessary. Fortunately, it's unlikely that they even know we're down here. I wish I had something better to say, but the time for grand speeches hasn't come yet. All you need to know is that I'm going up there and I'm leaving, no matter what I find."

Andie walked over to join the fighters, the Council, looking up at Marvo and thinking that what he was doing was brilliant. He knew as well as she did that the fighters were tapped, borderline hopeless, and trying to rally them in any traditional sense was futile. But everybody loved Marvo, and the easier, better option was to inspire them not to believe in themselves but to believe in him. Give a soldier orders and someone to look up to and their path becomes clear.

"I think they believe him," Yara said as she joined Andie among the now livelier-looking crowd.

"I hope so," Andie replied, threading her arm through Yara's extended elbow. "Whoever we find up there isn't going to be happy to see us. If we can't muster the courage to take them on, then we'll die in this tunnel. In the dark."

"Personally, I'm more concerned about what comes after that. Not only do we have to make it through the city and find somewhere safe, but we have to fight the lie. By now everyone up there thinks that your people are dangerous, evil. They must be so afraid, and you know what people are capable of when they're afraid. What kind of horrors are waiting for us up there? What kind of world are we going up to?"

"I don't know, but I suspect they won't be welcoming us back with open arms anytime soon. I just hope my people have managed to escape. I can't imagine how much this world has changed since their time. Everything must be so different to them now, and they have no one to trust. I just want to see them again."

"You will. Soon," Yara said, leaning her head against Andie's. She then gave her friend a brief hug and left to go help Carmen recover their packs and get ready for their journey back up to the surface.

Within an hour, everyone had rolled up what few things they had and was ready to go. Raesh seemed hopeful, or at least was trying his best to look so. Marvo now looked sullener than he had before, and Andie knew the toll all of this was taking on him. Just as she worried for the dragonborn, she knew Marvo worried for his fighters. They had risked so much in coming there to her aid. There were no speeches or last looks at the dark, cold place that had been their makeshift home, just a high signal from Marvo and then the moving of feet. Andie was the only one to look behind her and stare off into the deep dark of the cavern one final time.

The journey was slow, measured. Everyone was thinking the same thoughts and feeling the same fears, but it was eerily quiet as they walked. Carmen and Yara walked a few paces ahead of Andie, who walked side by side with Raesh, though even they were quiet. Andie nodded to both Kristole and Murakami, who had held up well even though they were the two oldest members of the group. Andie looked around her, took a serious look at the state they were in for the first time in a while.

They were thin, haggard, the men unshaved and the women's hair pulled back in loose, rough ponytails. All of the fighters wore black, but their clothes were horrendously dirty, frayed, and threadbare. Everybody walked slightly bent as if the invisible weight of the world was pulling their shoulders down. And although she couldn't see it with her eyes, she knew that they were all hungry and worn out inside. The battle at the University had been one fight, and living underground had been another. And, as much as it hurt Andie to think it, these fights were only just the beginning.

They may have won some battles, but they were still far off from winning the war.

CHAPTER THREE

It only took a few hours before they neared the surface. A muted, warm light flooded in from before them, and Andie could sense everyone's spirits rise immediately. Raesh had been sent ahead to scope out their exit, and Andie stood strong before the rest of the party, soaking in what little sunlight she could. Even the faint glow on her skin revitalized her, and she felt stronger than she had in months.

"It looks clear," Raesh said when he returned. "I didn't see or hear anything, but I don't like this at all. It doesn't feel right."

"I agree, son, but we don't have a choice. There's no way we can go back." Marvo paced back and forth as we all stood ready, waiting for his orders. Andie had stepped back and allowed Marvo to take over command. There was no one better than he to lead the group to victory, but she remained ready to step forward when the time came. Marvo turned back to face everyone and gave his commands. "Raesh, you stay up here at the front with me. I may need you and your pearlblood magic to blast through some things."

"Or some people," Raesh grinned. He looked like he was actually having fun, and Andie couldn't help but laugh. Raesh winked at her when he caught her staring, and a slight blush crept up her cheeks. She feigned a cough and turned the other way. It was definitely not time for flirting.

"Andie, I want you and Yara to bring up the rear. We don't need anything surprising us from behind. Carmen, you stay in the middle and try to be as light on that ankle as you can. Everybody stay in tight and stay ready. We're only going to get one shot at this."

"What do you think this is?" Yara asked.

The group looked around at one another, waiting for someone to answer. Andie rubbed her neck and let out a loud sign. "A trap," she finally said.

Silence swept through the tunnel at her words, but soon after everyone fell into position as Marvo directed. The fighters formed into a loose phalanx and Andie and Yara kept their heads up, looking for anything and everything. Andie had great instincts, and everything inside was telling her they had walked into something strange. It was simply too easy.

In a matter of moments, everyone had cleared the

edge of the tunnel, and they were above ground for the first time in months. But the farther they moved, the less sure Andie was. She tried to convince herself that their plan had worked, that the University had never known they were down there—after all, that was the point of their plan in the first place.

"Yara, how do you feel?"

"Like I'm going to be sick. My stomach is in knots."

"Good. Something isn't right. Don't do anything sudden, but get yourself ready. If they're going to attack it's going to be soo—"

Just as the words were leaving her mouth, a spell came from somewhere in the grand hallway and shattered the wall above the entrance to the tunnel. The debris fell in over the entrance and blocked it completely. Suddenly, people began to appear out of nowhere. Professors, Searchers, and some new adversary wearing all silver. Where before there had only been space and passageways, there were now dozens of enemies. They had apparently been using an invisibility spell. Andie looked in every direction, panic forming at the pit of her stomach. They were surrounded.

Time slowed for Andie. Suddenly she was thinking about all the questions she'd never have the chance to ask about her people. For all she knew they were dead already, and if they weren't, then it wouldn't be long before there was all out war. A thousand regrets passed through her mind as she gazed out at their enemies. They looked strong, fearless. She and her supporters were no match for these hateful people.

One of the silver-clad people moved forward, and Andie took a small step back. But as it came closer, Andie realized that it wasn't, in fact, a person dressed in silver at all. It looked to actually be *made* of silver. It wasn't human. It moved sedately, almost like a specter, yet it radiated danger and death. Andie could feel its magic radiating off it, an electric sting over her pale skin.

It moved to within a few feet of her and became still. Too still, as if all life had left it. Its mouth opened so wide that the rest of its face slid to the back of its head. Andie stood, paralyzed, staring into the blackness of the thing's mouth.

Its voice was metallic and void of all emotion. She had never met anything so inhuman in her life. "I am one of the twelve Sentinels. Forged in the furnaces of the Old World and reawakened now to restore peace."

The words were monotone, yet oddly hypnotic, no doubt spelled to mess with the mind of anyone who heard it. The thing that was hardest to comprehend was that as it spoke, its lips didn't move. It didn't even have lips. The sound simply came up from the center of it through its mouth. It was terribly unnerving.

"You and your fellow anarchists have been deemed enemies of the state, and it is only by your capture or execution that the land of Noelle may return to peace. You should choose your next step wisely." The mouth closed and the sentinel moved back to its post.

Andie tried to look to Marvo for a plan, but she couldn't see him. It didn't matter. She knew they didn't have time to compare notes and draw up a plan, but she did have her dragon magic. There was no point in hiding anymore since they were staring right at her. Quicker than the enemy could react, Andie raised her hands and pushed her magic out through space. She harnessed all the power she could muster, drawing on the energy she felt from the sunlight. Two great walls of lavender magic raced out to either side of her, crushing everything in their paths and destroying the walls of that room and the next three as well.

As the bodies flew and the dust and debris began to cloud the air, the Council began their attack. They erected shields to block the incoming hexes and created gaps through which they could cast in retaliation. The professors and Searchers hid behind the stone of the passageways and ducked the onslaught of magic. Raesh and Yara, despite how tired they must have been, cast furiously. Even Carmen pulled her strength together to fight.

They were making excellent progress, slowly continuing to inch forward as the spells flew all around. Andie, however, was barely able to stand. She hadn't quite noticed just how weak she was. Never realized how much the dragonborn needed warmth and sunlight. She had so much to learn about her people. The cold, damp, dark of the tunnels had been the worst possible place for her. The environment had sapped her even more than the constant hunger. The massive spell she had just done had taken a tremendous amount of what little strength she had left; it would have been nothing to her on a regular day, but now she felt weak, lightheaded. Yara sensed that something was wrong and caught Andie under her arm to support her.

"Hey, what's wrong?" she asked. "Andie, what's wrong?"

"Don't worry about me. Keep fighting."

"When your all-powerful best friend, who happens to be a member of one of the oldest and strongest races on earth, starts turning pale, something is wrong."

"I need the sun. I need warmth. I didn't know how depleted I was. I just need to get outside."

"And I'll get you there, I promise. Just stay on your feet."

Yara took on a new ferocity then, supporting Andie with one arm and casting with the other. Marvo was nearby, fighting like a wild man. He'd run out of ammo the night of the Winter Festival, and now he was getting in close for combat, and despite his age, he was too much for the professors who only knew how to fight with magic. The group was almost around the corner of the hall; all they needed to do was fight through a dozen professors.

Just when they were nearly through, though, three of the Sentinels dashed in front of them, no longer sedated and unbelievably quick. They stood there, silent and still, and waited for the group to come to them. The fighters began casting at the Sentinels, but the beings moved too quickly. One of the Sentinels reached forward, and its arm stretched ten feet and pierced right through Kristole. Andie screamed as she tried to call on her strength to help, but the older woman was dead before she hit the ground.

The other Sentinels changed their shape, made themselves bigger and began to knock the fighters aside with incredible force. With every hit, she could hear bones breaking. The Sentinels were merciless. Raesh turned to one that was moving in to attack him and tried to defend, but the Sentinel was too quick. It knocked him back several feet and then raced to hit him before he stood. Raesh rolled out of the way and came back to his feet. He cast a spell, missed, and was hit so hard he shook dust from the walls. Yara was about to release Andie to go help when Raesh unleashed his frenzied, unbridled magic and ripped right through the Sentinel in a brilliant blaze of yellow light. As the Sentinel flew back, Raesh looked to Andie with the widest grin on his face she had ever seen.

Andie looked all around her and saw the carnage that had fallen on them. She knew there were only a few moments left before the end. She gathered every ounce of strength she had left and pushed Yara aside. One of the Sentinels had liquefied itself and then completely submerged one of the fighters. It was impossible to tell exactly what had happened. As it turned to Andie, she raised her hands in front of her.

"Everybody down!" she yelled.

The fighters ducked, and Andie sent out the hottest, brightest flame she could muster. The two remaining Sentinels were blown back and incinerated in the air before they could even fall back to the floor. She had saved her friends. The enemies withdrew, but she felt herself falling backward, leaving, disappearing.

Then darkness.

"GET HER UP, we have to move!"

The sound of running feet. So many running feet.

"Lookout, there's more of the— "

"Hold her, come on, faster, faster— "

Speed. Gravity. The world sliding by at a sheer angle and the green-tinted rain pounding across space.

"There's too many of them!"

"Everybody run for the front! Don't get left be— "

Crashing. Something huge and fast and dangerous crashing. The world is tilting, turning, tumbling.

"Is he dead? Turn him ov— "

The soft falls of the thick rain. Feet hitting water. Yelling.

"Yara! Raesh!"

"Coming up from behind!"

A ship.

WHEN ANDIE WOKE, she didn't know what time or even what day it was. She looked around and didn't know where she was. The only things she recognized were Raesh sitting in a chair across from her and Yara in the bed next to her. The room was small, brightly painted, and simply furnished. It didn't take her long to realize that the room was lolling gently from side to side. They were on a ship. She was more confused than ever. The only things that brought her comfort were her friends and the sunlight streaming in through the open window, though the window was small. She turned over and lay her hand on Yara's shoulder. Yara woke with a start.

"Andie! Are you okay? How do you feel?" Yara pushed herself up on the bed and looked down at Andie with concern in her eyes.

"Better. A lot better," Andie said. She stretched out her arms and realized what she said was true. She felt totally fine. "Whose ship are we on?"

"The Council's," Yara said through a yawn. "Turns out they're a lot bigger than we thought they were. They've got factions all over west Noelle. They were waiting for us at a port on the coast of Arvall."

Andie sat bolt upright. "What? Why didn't Marvo tell us he had a plan? Where is he?"

"He was injured in the escape, but they say he'll pull through. Andie, I have to tell you something."

Yara took Andie's hand and looked in her eyes. Andie knew that whatever was coming was going to hurt.

"The enemy knew we were coming."

CHAPTER FOUR

A<small>NDIE</small> <small>STARED</small> <small>AT</small> Y<small>ARA</small> <small>FOR</small> <small>A</small> <small>LONG</small> <small>MOMENT</small> <small>BEFORE</small> she spoke. "What do you mean, they knew we were coming? No one knew we were down there."

Yara shook her head and rubbed her eyes with the palms of her hands. "They knew we were coming, Andie."

"But how?"

Yara simply stared at her until comprehension dawned on Andie's face. "You mean someone betrayed us? How?"

"I don't know, but I suspect it's why Marvo didn't tell any of us about the ship," Yara said. "He'd been trying to smoke them out weeks before the battle in the Archives, but nothing ever happened, and he thought maybe he'd misjudged. But he started to get suspicious again after we hid in the tunnels. Someone had been throwing away our rations from the scavenging trips. And even if the University had known we were down there, there was no way they could have known exactly when we'd come up. Somebody told them to be ready to ambush us."

"Well, who is it?" Andie asked, disbelieving. "Who betrayed us?" The idea that one of their own was a traitor made her feel sick to her stomach. After everything they had been through together, she couldn't imagine any of them turning their back to the cause.

"We don't know. We lost some people in the escape, but whoever it is must be on the ship with us. The University wouldn't hurt them and risk losing an informant if we got away."

"Did you see anyone in the fight who wasn't being targeted?"

"No. Did you?"

"No. I have to find Marvo. We need to find this person now."

"Wait," Yara said, pointing to Raesh. "Let him rest. Let's talk outside."

The girls got up and quietly moved around Raesh until they were outside. They walked down several hallways, and they exited up onto the lower deck. Andie's body was still healing, and the moment the direct sunlight touched her, she began to fill with energy, power. It felt amazing.

"I don't know if I can believe it," Andie finally said as they leaned against the wooden deck rails. She stared out into the open ocean, curious where they were headed but not wanting to change the subject before she found out the truth about their traitor. The sea breeze sprayed salt water over her skin as she stood there in silence, contemplating what Yara had told her. Andie squeezed her eyes shut as she thought, relishing in the warmth of the sun and the refreshing sea air.

"Andie, I know how you feel," said Yara, looking out over the sea. "We have to keep this to ourselves for now, though."

"Are you kidding me? No way. I have to find out who did this to us. How many people did you say we lost?"

Yara shook her head. "I didn't. Right now, it doesn't matter."

Andie turned to her friend, her eyes flashing with anger. "Of course, it matters. Every single person here matters. I have to know who would betray us like this."

"Please, Andie. Promise me you'll stay quiet. Just for now."

"Are you insane? I'm not letting us go another minute with a traitor amongst us. Whoever it is could be using a hundred different methods of invisible communication to talk to the University. We have to do something now."

"Andie, there's no way to tell who it is. If they've been in the Council this long, they're obviously good at pretending."

"It must have been someone doing scavenging missions."

"Andie, we were all doing scavenging missions. And almost all of us have done at least one solo mission. Look, Marvo took a huge risk in telling me. The only people we know it can't be are you, me, and Marvo."

"And Carmen and Raesh."

"We hope Carmen and Raesh."

Andie couldn't even respond. She just stared at Yara, dumbfounded.

"Don't look at me like that, Andie. You know Marvo wants to trust his own family, but this thing is too big to leave to chance or love. We have to be one hundred percent sure before we even think of giving anyone the benefit of the doubt."

"Let's just find Marvo."

Andie didn't say a word as Yara lead her through the halls. It wasn't until they reached the rooms that Andie began to greet and check on the fighters. Carmen was sleeping, having finally gotten her ankle properly seen to. The ship was much bigger than Andie had anticipated, and there were fighters stationed everywhere. Andie couldn't help giving them all a cold stare when they weren't looking; any one of them could have been the spy. When they reached Marvo's room, he was sitting up in bed, a bandage covering most of the right side of his face and several smaller bandages in various places across his arms. Andie had to take a breath when she saw him. Yara went to sit in the corner.

"Easy, Andie," he said. "I'm perfectly fine, aside from some minor scrapes. There's a lot of them, but nothing too serious. I'll heal…"

Andie took an angry step forward and opened her mouth to scold him for not trusting his own family, but Marvo held up his hands and spoke before she got a word out.

"… And before you berate me for not trusting Raesh and Carmen, just trust that I've thought it out and that it's even harder for me than it is for you. Now have a seat, we've got some catching up to do."

Andie stared at him incredulously for a long moment, then finally let out a loud sigh and pulled a chair up to his bedside. She took Marvo's hand and waited for him to start, holding her own words in until she fully understood what he had to say.

"First, we've been branded enemies of the state. Not just Arvall City, but all of Noelle. There are wanted posters of our faces up for thousands of leagues, and who knows whatever else around the entire rest of Shaeyara outside the boundaries of Noelle. You don't even want to know how much the reward for our heads is. If we're caught, that's it. We'll be executed the same day. We've got to be more than careful in the coming weeks."

The news didn't surprise Andie. She had figured as much was happening from the first day they entered the caverns below ground eight months before. "What else?"

"We still don't have any word on your people. There were some sightings in north central Noelle, but that was months ago. But no news is good news because it means—"

"They haven't been captured yet," Andie finished.

Marvo nodded. "Exactly. It seems they've evaded capture so far. We've barely even heard whispers of their potential whereabouts."

"They're probably headed somewhere with mountains. That's where they'd be most comfortable. I haven't tried reaching out to Saeryn in a while, but maybe I could—"

"Trust me, Andie, for now, let them hide. We'll find them when the time is right. We've been lucky so far. I had my people waiting at the docks the night of the battle, thinking we'd come straight out. But when we decided to stay inside, they stayed at the dock and waited."

"Who are these friends of yours?"

"Just more people on our side, Andie. But never mind about that. The University is going to reopen, and it's going to be more dangerous than ever. They're planning on becoming a military training facility, and that means their sole focus will be teaching sorcerers how to excel at war. And they've vowed to rid the earth of the world's greatest enemy: the dragonborn."

The words felt like poison in her ears. As if the world wasn't toxic enough, the University was now going to add strength to their hatred. Andie could hardly believe how cruel and unjust the world could be.

"There's already been a formal declaration of war," Yara said from the corner. "From what we can tell it was met with rousing applause in the streets. They've certainly done a good job of convincing the world of the dragonborn's evil. The only way to save us now is to reunite you with your people and try to convince the entire world that the dragonborn aren't a threat."

"Fat chance," Andie said with a humorless laugh.

"You don't know how right you are," Marvo said, squeezing her hand. "When we were running through the streets, we saw the city burning. Raids, attacks, more desperate people than I've ever seen in my life. Complete and utter carnage. And you wouldn't believe what kinds of hateful propaganda the University is putting out. The most awful things you can think of. They're calling you and your people a plague."

"We're running out of time."

"We may already be out of time."

"I guess I understand that. Where are we headed now?"

"To the True Isles. I know you've never been so I won't try to describe it to you, except to say that if you ever wondered what paradise looked like, you're about to find out."

"And what's in the True Isles? More allies?"

"Yes, and hopefully a way to get those icons out of you girls. For all we know the University could be tracking us now."

"True. Well, if we get rid of them that will be one less thing to worry about. How far are the isles form Michaelson? I want to see my dad."

"Andie," Marvo began, sitting up and looking away. "I can't let you go there."

"Are you out of your mind? What do you think they'll do if they catch him? They'll torture him for information!"

"Andie, calm down and think. We've been underground for months. If they had wanted your father, they could have found him and killed him by now."

Andie closed her eyes and shuddered. She couldn't bear the thought of anything happening to him, especially not after she had been so lax in staying in touch with him in the weeks before they went into hiding. She didn't know what she'd do if anything had happened to him.

"As it happens, I'd already sent people to get him the night of the battle. Hopefully, they're still at the safe location I established. We've already sent word for them to meet us in the True Isles. I know it's not ideal, but this is the safest way."

Andie nodded slowly. The slow sway of the ship calmed her, made her feel somehow grounded, strangely enough. "I understand."

"Speaking of safety, I've said all I can say to you about what's ahead for us."

"Meaning?" Andie crossed her arms and stared back at Marvo, a look of sheer indignation in her eyes.

"Meaning I trust that you're not our spy, but I don't trust that you won't talk to Raesh and Carmen about the things you just heard."

She couldn't believe that not only was there a traitor among them but that Marvo could ever in a million years consider that Carmen and Raesh couldn't be trusted. Being thorough was one thing, but not trusting the two of them was ridiculous. Her anger was mitigated by how much it hurt her to see him laid up like that. Andie didn't even bother responding. She stood and was already out in the hall before she turned around to face Marvo and Yara.

"Fine. You sit there and be suspicious of everyone, of your own blood, and I'll go on trusting the people who have repeatedly risked their lives for me."

Marvo began to speak, but Andie was out of the room before he could say a word.

CHAPTER FIVE

ANDIE WALKED THE LOWER DECK SIX TIMES BEFORE she could bring herself to relax. She tried her best to see the situation from Marvo's angle, but she just couldn't wrap her brain around what he was doing. She finally settled towards the back of the deck and leaned over the rail, looking down into the roiling depths of the ocean they traveled through. The misty salt air made her skin itch, but she ignored the sensation and tilted her head back, basking in the warmth of the sun.

She tried to reason with herself, considering why Marvo might not trust those closest to him. It wasn't so uncommon for sorcerers to use spells to control people's mind and make them do whatever they wanted. Raesh and Carmen could be doing someone else's bidding against their will. She realized Marvo was probably right in his secrecy, as perhaps their traitor wasn't even intentionally betraying them. Someone could be acting against their will. Trapped in their own mind.

Andie sighed loudly and rubbed her eyes. The idea that one of her own, possibly even one of her closest friends, could be being controlled by the enemy made her stomach tie up in knots. She gritted her teeth in determination, clear at what she must do. She had to discover the traitor as soon as possible. She couldn't waste any time.

The winds picked up, and the water began splashing up more violently, and Andie began pacing again, trying to think back to when someone could have been spelled. If that was in fact what happened, it must have been an exceptionally powerful spell to have lasted that whole time. She didn't even know anyone powerful enough to have set such a spell, even at the University. She so desperately wanted to believe whoever betrayed them did it against their own will, but her instinct told her otherwise.

She finally settled down enough to realize how beautiful the view was. She stopped and leaned on the railing. She'd only seen the Spider Sea once before, but never from a ship. The sun was falling into the horizon, and the sky overhead was like a chest full of gold that someone had tossed across the black of space. And below, the sea was endless, already beginning to be dappled with the light of the trench spiders. They were coming up from the caves, where they rest during the day, to play near the surface of the sea during the night.

The water seemed ten times darker than it was when they came up and brought the incredible silver light of their bodies. Trench spiders looked similar to the spiders on land, only about twenty times bigger and their eight legs were like eight long feathers. Their thorax looked like a dandelion. Andie couldn't help but notice how stunning they were, thousands upon thousands of those little silver lights coming up from the trenches as far as the eye could see.

"They're kind of incredible."

Andie was startled by the voice, but it was only Raesh. He looked well, like he hadn't been hurt much during the escape, but Andie wasn't really surprised. Raesh's magic couldn't be controlled like hers could, but he was still extremely powerful, and he was learning how to use his particular kind of magic to his advantage. She was so busy looking him over for injuries that it took her a moment to realize he was smiling at her. She smiled back.

"I see you came out practically unscathed," she said.

"With the exception of a few bruised ribs and a smattering of completely not serious cuts. My dad got it a little worse, I think. But, he'll be fine."

"Speaking of your dad. I just spoke with him and Yara."

"And I can tell by the tone of your voice that he told you about the traitor and certain people who have yet to be ruled off his list of suspects?"

"He told you about that? You mean he actually told you to your face that he didn't trust you?"

"Well, it wasn't quite like that. You have to understand, he's being thorough. You and he are our leaders and, honestly, neither of you can afford to make any kind of move without thinking of every possible outcome. I know he wants to trust me, but he has to look out for so many people now. And, you know, for all he knows, I could be one hundred percent loyal to him, but be under a professor's spell or something."

Andie stared at him for a minute but eventually relented.

"I know," she said, running her hands through her hair in frustration. "I had the same thought, as well. I just can't believe this is happening. How could one of our own friends do this to us? It's unreal. And maybe Marvo is a leader, but Yara should know you two well enough to give you the benefit of the doubt."

"Maybe you should cut her some slack."

"For what? You gonna tell me she's a leader, too?"

"In her defense, she caught Carmen and me talking about some things."

"Like what? What could make her doubt you two? What, were you planning to capture me and render me powerless?"

Raesh looked away and didn't respond. Andie waited and watched him, feeling her joke lose its humor dramatically as the seconds passed.

"Raesh?"

"You have to understand, Andie. You're the most powerful person we know. Maybe one of the most powerful in the world."

"I think that's a bit of an over exaggeration, Raesh," Andie snorted.

"No, I'm serious. You're both sorceress and dragonborn. I've searched the records, and I don't think there's been anyone else like you... ever."

Andie blinked and stared at him a long moment, but she supposed she hadn't heard of another like her, either.

"And we don't even know the extent of what your dragonblood can do," Raesh continued. "Andie, you can fly. You can make lightning stronger, brighter, and hotter than anything I've ever seen. Your body can heal any injury. There might not even be a limit to your power. We know, beyond anything, you would never willingly betray us, but if you were ever to fall under the control of one of the professors or anyone else... I don't know if we'd ever be able to stop you."

Andie considered him a moment and then nodded. "I suppose you're right."

"It was only a list of possible contingency plans," Raesh said. When Andie turned to look at him, her eyes blazing, he quickly added, "None of which we kept, by the way. But, Yara happened to overhear us. I think deep down she knows we'd never do it unless we had to, but it really shook her up, and I guess I never realized how much."

"I see," Andie said, turning from him to the sea.

They stared out at nothing for nearly ten minutes, letting the silence fill them as they thought about the relationships and potential in their lives. Finally, Andie sighed.

"I'm sorry, Raesh. I know it's something no one wants to admit, but something we all should be worried about. If anybody ever figured out how to control me, it would be... catastrophic. And, if I'm being honest, I guess what really has me so freaked out is passing out during the escape."

"What do you mean?"

"It's humiliating."

"Don't even start with that," Raesh said, turning to her. "You're dragonborn. You need the sun to stay strong, and none of us even knew that. You'd been underground for eight months. If you weren't so powerful, you wouldn't have even been able to do as much as you did. You took out two of those Sentinels. You're the reason we survived."

"Well, in the interest of giving credit where credit is due, you took out one yourself. What were those things anyway?"

"I have no freaking clue. No one has ever even heard of them. It did say it was from the Old World. Whatever they are, they're powerful. Incredibly powerful."

"I don't remember what happened after I took down those two. Who all did we lose?"

"By the time we made it outside, there weren't many of us left. We ran as fast as we could, and my dad and I carried you. The Searchers chased us and never stopped firing. We lost another on the way out."

"How did we escape?"

"We made it to SKY 6 and took over the train. We started down Brie and, for a while, we thought we were safe, but the Searchers had got on the train, too, and they brought five more of those Sentinels with them. We couldn't really fight them off. There weren't enough of us then, and you were unconscious."

"Raesh," Andie tried to make out the expression on Raesh's face, but he stared out at the setting sun, his face as blank as she had ever seen it. "I'm so sorry I wasn't able to help."

Raesh didn't even seem to hear her. He continued

as if she hadn't even spoke. "We lost two more in the fighting. One of the Searchers set the train on fire with his gun, and then the train started to shake. The gravity control gave out. Before we knew it, we were all floating, but it gave us the upper hand. We managed to take out all of the Searchers, but the Sentinels were too strong. They killed two more of us and hurt my dad."

"I…"

"The only thing that saved us from them was the same thing that almost killed us. The train went off the rails. Yara and Carmen locked us all in a protective shell. The Sentinels almost broke through their magic, but they were thrown as the train cars tumbled, flipped, and raced down the mountain. Everything was tearing apart around us. Crashing, exploding, being ripped away. We finally landed at the bottom, half alive, but away from the Sentinels. Luckily, my dad's friends were still waiting by the sea. And we escaped."

"That sounds incredibly terrifying. Raesh, I'm so sorry I couldn't help. I'm sorry I wasn't strong enough to…"

"Andie, stop."

"I'm sorry."

"It was a nightmare. But we made it."

"Yeah, you did. And you saved me, too."

She gave Raesh's shoulder a squeeze, and he finally looked back at her as if he had been pulled away from a dream. He looked haunted, but he smiled back.

"I guess I did."

LATER THAT NIGHT as Andie was lying in her bed, restless beyond anything imaginable, she heard the door open behind her. She turned over to see who it was. Yara. Yara first walked into the room, and then took a step back and leaned on the open doorway. Andie could tell she had something she wanted to say, but after the cold shoulders they'd exchanged earlier, it was difficult for them to face each other.

Andie turned back over, hoping Yara would talk herself out of whatever half apology she was thinking up just then. For a long time, Yara sat staring at the wall, not speaking, not moving, hardly even breathing, and Andie lay in her bed, trying desperately to fall into the sleep she knew would never come when she wanted it.

"You think you've got it all figured out."

Andie grew angry almost instantly. If Yara had come to apologize, it would have been bad enough, but to come into the room in the middle of the night and accuse her? And exactly what was she accusing her of?

"You can lie there and pretend to be asleep or pretend that you can't hear me. It'll only make this easier. You think that because we're all here together and we have a history that we can all be trusted. Given the benefit of the doubt outright. Well, that's the definition of a traitor, Andie. Someone you trust. Someone you would never suspect in a million years."

Andie lay still, listening. The gentle sway of the ship rocked them back and forth, the sound of the ocean on the other side of the smooth wooden walls a muted rhythm that Andie hoped would lull her to sleep.

"The University is smart, so smart," Yara continued. "They know who matters to you most and who you would blindly put your faith in. All Marvo and I are trying to do is protect the more than five hundred lives on this ship, including yours. And I'll pretend I didn't notice when you forgave Marvo practically immediately and yet you won't even turn over now to look at me. Whatever."

Andie sighed and turned towards the doorway where Yara stood with her arms crossed. Her expression smoldering in the dim light. "Yara…"

"But it doesn't matter," Yara interrupted. "I'm still your friend. I'm still your ally. I'm still the girl you asked to come along on this impossible mission with you because you knew that I would always do the right thing."

"I asked Carmen, too."

"Well, Carmen isn't cleared yet. It's like you're not even listening to me!"

Yara pushed herself away from the door and paced for a bit. Andie curled herself up even more, grabbing the pillow up around her head in a fruitless effort to get more comfortable. After a few minutes of pacing angrily, Yara threw herself onto her bed.

"I've been in Arvall City for the last ten years. Since I was sixteen. But I wasn't always there. I was born on the other side of Noelle. It was a small town, a village really. It didn't even have a name. It was like it was the place that time forgot. That everything forgot. But we were happy there. We didn't have much, but we had each other."

Andie tried to read Yara's face, but she simply stared up at the ceiling, refusing to meet Andie's gaze.

"Actually, we were pretty poor. Unbelievably poor. But so was everybody else." Yara spoke slowly, as if recalling a painful memory that she had hoped to forget. "For a long time, I didn't even recognize that we didn't have money or nice things, but the older I got, the more I began to understand that we weren't okay, that we had nothing. And I remember I would get so angry when I looked around our house, or what was left of it, and see that we were living like... like I don't even know what. So, I started to steal. Little things at first. Bananas, potatoes, towels. Things we needed to survive. My mother would ask where they came from and I would lie, saying people gave them to me or I found them or I earned them from doing jobs around the village. But soon I grew bored. I wanted more. So, I started stealing other things. Money. Family heirlooms. Clothes. Things we didn't need, but I wanted. But that wasn't enough either."

"Why are you telling me this?" Andie asked, but Yara ignored her question.

"I started sneaking around the big cities that were to the north of us. And by then I was good. I was the best. You can't imagine all the things I had. Money, jewelry, more food and clothes and things than I could use in a lifetime. And then one day I decided never to go home again. To stay in the city and live the life I thought I deserved. I was only fifteen, but people care less about your age and more about what you can do for them when you have the skillset I did. And so, I left."

"Yara…"

"My parents came looking for me. My connections told me they were getting close, so I hid away where they would never find me," Yara continued. "A few months passed. I came out again, and I found out that they had never left. They'd stayed in the city, living in an alley behind the apartment I'd been staying in. Some gang was doing their business in the alley and my parents were just there and happened to see it. And so, they killed them. They slaughtered my parents right there in the alley like they were nothing. Of course, they did it with magic, and the police didn't have the resources to track that kind of attack. And it was days before anybody even noticed the smell and found the bodies."

"I'm so sorry," Andie whispered. She had no idea her friend's life had been so dark.

"It was strange. All I had to do was go down and see them. Talk to them. Tell them I didn't want to go home, that I could provide for all three of us there in the city. And it wasn't even them I was running away from. It was poverty. It was hunger and cold and fear. I just wanted to feel safe in my own life."

Andie didn't know what to say. Yara was opening up about her past for the first time, saying things Andie never could have imagined. She didn't know how to react. She loosened the ball she'd made of herself and turned over to her other side so that she faced Yara completely. Yara was still staring up at the ceiling. Her eyes seemed lost, her face blank and her eyes hurt. Andie was about to speak, even if it was just to mumble some trite expression, but she stopped herself, sensing Yara wasn't finished.

"By then I knew I was a sorceress and that I was pretty powerful, so I practiced my magic and learned as many spells as I could remember. It took me almost a year before I thought I was ready. And then I found them. The gang. With my connections, it didn't take long. By then I was sixteen and legal. I didn't have to sneak around anymore. I followed them to their hideout…"

Yara paused. The waves against the ship's hull below now nearly deafening in the silence that threatened to consume the room.

"…and I killed them."

Andie felt her entire body go tense. She wondered if she'd heard correctly. Did her best friend just admit to being a murderer?

"It was the worst mistake I ever made in my life. Even now, ten years later, it haunts me. Every time I do magic or think about fighting the University, I remember those men. The way they looked when I was finished with them. Andie, you have to understand that I don't think I'm above you or Carmen or Raesh. Or anyone else. I don't think I've earned your trust or your friendship. But I know what can happen to a person when they come under strain. True, honest strain."

Yara finally turned to look at Andie, her eyes darker and more haunted than Andie had ever seen. "You don't have to be evil to be capable of it. All I want is to make sure that every person on this ship is still intact and then find the one person on this ship who's broken. So, no, I'm not going to trust someone's intentions just because I know them. And yes, I will make it my duty to personally assess Raesh and Carmen before they're cleared. And you can hate me for that, but I don't really care."

Andie stared incredulously at her but finally nodded. Yara nodded back and returned her gaze back up to the ceiling.

"And one last thing," Yara added. "I abandoned my parents, and they died. I won't abandon this group. Not in any way. Not ever."

Yara leaned back in the bed, covered herself fully with her blankets, and lay there silently. Andie stared at her for several moments, trying to figure out what to say or if she was supposed to say anything at all. But before she could come up with anything appropriate to say, Yara had fallen asleep.

CHAPTER SIX

THE NEXT DAY WAS A LITTLE BETTER FOR EVERYONE onboard. The chaos of the escape was a little further behind them, but the traitor still had everyone terrified. They didn't know if the person was just giving information to the University, or if he or she had orders to kill them in their sleep. Everyone was suspicious of everyone except their closest friends, and so divisions grew up overnight. Even then, no one liked to be surrounded by more than three people at a time. Tensions were high, maybe even insurmountable. Rumors of who the traitor could be spread faster than wildfire, and Andie had had just about enough.

Andie was meeting with the captain that morning. They'd already docked in the True Isles, but the order had come up from Marvo that no one was to leave the ship yet. Andie had spent half the morning trying to comprehend the story Yara had told her and trying to separate how she felt about Yara's past from how she felt about Yara now. She'd spent the other half of the morning thinking of where the dragonborn might go for safety. Both dragons and dragonborn preferred mountainous regions if the history books were to be believed. She certainly felt like it could be true.

Brie was the highest mountain by far, but there was no way they would ever go back there. It would be too dangerous. They had been spotted most recently over Abhainn, which was almost the geographical center of Noelle. She hoped they would be smart enough to seek safety elsewhere.

"You don't have anything more specific than that?" the captain asked.

"I might," Andie said. "Where's your map?"

"Hanging up there."

He walked with her over to a wall-length window, and Andie saw that it was actually a massive map of the world. It was completely made of loveglass, and shimmered with an iridescent glow. The captain touched the map and the glass changed, zoomed in to show only Noelle. It was controlled by a combination of the user's magic and the geographic data fed to it through the comm station. It was fascinating, and Andie stared at it as if seeing loveglass for the first time.

"What, never seen a loveglass map before?" the captain grinned.

Andie shook her head and walked up to the map, narrowing it to the regions surrounding Abhainn with her own magic. "It's incredible."

"Pretty basic stuff, really," the captain said proudly. "But I've never seen a map so big as this one. Have had it in my care for the past ten years, I'd reckon."

Andie smiled and quickly steered the conversation back to the matter at hand. "The dragons were last spotted here," she said, pointing to the map. The captain deflated somewhat, but turned his attention dutifully back to Andie. She narrowed her eyes as she inspected the map closely. "Now it looks like there are at least six different mountain ranges nearby. We don't know which way they were heading, but these two here don't have the elevation they'd want, even in these circumstances. That one at the top is too far north; it wouldn't be warm enough for the dragons."

"Leaving the three to the southwest here," said the captain. "I know for a fact that middle one has been taken over by the Glycerinnds after they fled from Brie. Now I know pirates, even a few hundred of them, are no match for your people, but I'm assuming they wouldn't be looking to cause trouble or start something that could alert the public to where they are?"

"You'd be right. That leaves these two."

"So, which is it?"

Andie sighed. "I don't know. They both have the right elevation, the right temperature. They're secluded. It's hard to tell."

"How do we even know they're still in this region? They were spotted here, but they could've gone anywhere. Noelle is almost twenty-three thousand leagues from coast to coast."

"No, if they were spotted here it means they were coming down to land. Dragons can fly near the very outer layers of the atmosphere, too high to ever be seen from the ground. If someone saw them, it was because they'd found somewhere to land. But where?"

Andie and the captain sat looking over the map, but it wasn't long before an idea come to her.

"This one. That's where they are."

The captain tapped the glass and the mountain range Andie selected was brought up.

"That's in the Hot Salts of Mithraldia," he said. "I guess it'd be hot enough. But wait... lightning is constant there, sometimes several thousand times per hour. The clouds never clear there. Don't your people need sun?"

"Exactly. If these were the only two viable ranges in the area, they must've known that eventually someone would put the pieces together and go looking for them. Now both of these mountain ranges are large enough that it would take even a sizable team a long while to search the whole thing, but eventually someone would find them. No one would think to look for them near the Hot Salts, under a constant cloudy sky. They'll be growing weak, but they could fly above the weather to the sun whenever they really needed it."

The captain sat back in his chair, looking over Andie with a smile of pride on his face. When she looked back to him, he furrowed his brow and looked back to the map. "The lightning can be treacherous. Are you sure that's where they'd be?"

"They're there, I'm sure of it."

"Alright. I'll get the new heading into the system."

"Thank you, captain."

The captain nodded and immediately set to work inputting coordinates into the ship's navigation system. Andie watched him work meticulously at the wheel for a moment, and knew the ship was in good hands. With one last look back to the captain, she turned and left and went back out onto the deck, where Carmen was waiting for her with two bottles of something extremely bright.

"What is it?" Andie asked, taking the one Carmen handed her.

"Believe it or not, beer. It's good, take my word for it. I'm on my fourth."

"Your fourth?" Andie laughed, looking Carmen up

and down. Carmen's legs wobbled slightly beneath her, but she quickly steadied herself on the nearby wall. The girls turned their bottles up and started walking back downstairs.

"So," Carmen began. "How long is it going to take us to get to this mystery location?"

Andie turned to looked at Carmen from the side of her eye.

"Oh, I see. No one can trust the spy. God forbid I send this top secret info back to my clandestine buddies at headquarters."

"Carmen…"

"Nope, understandable. Must keep everything in ship shape. Lips sealed, files locked, legs closed, the usual."

"Carmen…"

"But you should know now that I actually do plan on killing you slowly, painfully in your bed tonight. I mean, nothing personal, orders and what not. It's all very straightforward, really. Wouldn't do it if it weren't absolutely necessary. I mean, you are the enemy, after all."

"Carmen," Andie said, laughing. "You're being ridiculous. You know I trust you. And you know that deep down Marvo trusts you, too."

Carmen sighed and chugged the rest of her beer, wiping the dripping liquid from her lips with her sleeve. "I know. To be honest, it's kind of refreshing to not have some giant weight resting on my shoulders."

"You mean, minus the fact that we're trying to save my entire species from extinction and evil rumors. Not to mention we can't use magic because the University is tracking us using technology we're going to have to have surgically removed?"

Carmen grinned. "Yeah. Minus that. Thanks for the reminder."

The girls laughed as they continued down the hall together.

"So, is there anything you *can* tell me?"

"Well, Carmen... you're still pretty."

"Now we're talking."

Carmen put her arm around Andie's shoulder. They only had a few minutes before they needed to be at the meeting. Raesh had called a meeting to explain a system for the division of information so that no one person knew everything. The girls rounded the corner and passed two rooms before they reached the mess hall. They went inside and it was nearly completely full of Marvo's fighters. Andie hadn't realized there were so many onboard.

"Wow," Carmen said. "I guess we don't need to be worried about an attack. There must be four or five hundred people in here."

"Now if we only knew the *one* person who we can't trust."

Carmen looked at Andie and they shared a concerned look.

"That's funny, I just had an even more terrifying thought," said Carmen.

"What?" Andie asked, not really wanting to hear another reason to worry.

"How do we know it's only one spy?"

Andie shook her head, wondering why Carmen had even said that. She knew she wouldn't be getting any sleep when the time came, but she couldn't afford to worry about those things now.

"I don't see Yara," Andie said, changing the subject. "Although, I guess even if she was in here, it'd take me forever to find her. I can't believe how many people are on this ship. We've still got some time. Wanna check to make sure?"

"Yeah. We could probably find her with Marvo. She's becoming quite the introvert."

Andie and Carmen started off down the hall again. What Carmen had said was true; Yara had had lost all social skills and desire overnight, it seemed. Andie hadn't noticed it when she first woke up, but the more time she spent around Yara, the more she realized that her friend had grown to distrust everyone. The knowledge of a traitor among them had had a heavy effect on her, not to mention the conversation she'd overheard between Carmen and Raesh. She wouldn't eat in the mess hall or talk to anyone. Raesh said she had been like that ever since Marvo told her there was a spy onboard.

Yara was almost always near Marvo, discussing and planning, or up in the crow's nest looking down on all the passengers and taking notes on their groups, behaviors, preferences, etc. She talked to Andie and Marvo, seldom to Raesh and Carmen, and never to anyone else. Besides all of that, Andie was certain there were other things bothering her, too. Probably the weight of her circumstance finally catching up to her.

Andie and Carmen reached Marvo's room. Murakami was standing guard at the door. She'd sustained some injuries during the escape, but only one serious one that Andie could see. A grisly slash that began at her temple and ran down to her chest. Andie hadn't had a chance to speak with her since they boarded, but by the concentrated look on the woman's face, she suspected it wasn't the best time to chit chat.

"Murakami," she said, touching the woman's shoulder. "How are you?"

"A lot worse than the Sentinel who did this to me, but I'll survive. Glad to see you're up. It's better for the cause that you're conscious."

"Thanks, I think. Are you sure you don't want that bandaged? It looks deep."

"No medicine, no bandage. Where I come from

stiches are enough. The pain is real. The rest of you can try avoiding it, but it reminds me of everything that's at stake."

"I understand. I know you're not doing this just because of me, Murakami, but I just want to say thank you for being here, and I'm sorry for the friends you lost."

"So am I."

Murakami didn't say anything else or turn away, but there was a certain kind of finality in her voice that told Andie the conversation should end there. She gave Murakami a smile as the woman moved aside. Andie opened the door and she and Carmen walked in. Yara was in there, so were three fighters who had been with them since the battle in the Archives. Their names were Kent, Sarinda, and Lilja.

Yara seemed her usual closed-off self, but Marvo was finally on his feet again. In fact, there was another person in his bed. Andie moved to congratulate Marvo on being able to stand, but just as she was touching his arm she got around Sarinda and saw who was in Marvo's bed. She couldn't move. She couldn't believe it.

"Dad?"

CHAPTER SEVEN

A RAGING, HEAD-POUNDING THUNDER PULLED ANDIE into consciousness.

It came again and again, relentless, so close but yet so far away. Something sharp was pressing into the side of her face and her leg was cold. Too cold. She tried to open her eyes, but when she finally did something immediately covered them. Her eyes started to burn. She tried to pick herself up, but she couldn't move her arms and she soon found she couldn't move her legs either. It was like she was frozen in the middle of something thick and strong. She couldn't breathe, there was no light, and no sound. She was all alone, or at least she thought she was. She couldn't tell. The booming noise got louder, and Andie thought it was perhaps an oncoming storm until she realized it was the sound of her own heart beat raging loudly in her ears.

She struggled and struggled, but could do no more than manage to wiggle a little. Before she'd thought she was lying down, but now she knew she was neither lying nor standing. She tasted blood and soil and an immense pressure built over her skin. She was suspended. In dirt.

Finally, it dawned on her exactly where she was. She was buried. Someone had tried to bury her alive. She felt weak, like she'd been out of the sun for a while. She considered, but it couldn't have been more than a few seconds. It was only moments ago that she was on the ship, surrounded by people she knew. Her father.

Panic threatened to overtake her, but she forced her mind to remain calm as she puzzled out her situation. Her thunderous heart beat grew louder still, and the pressure in her head built. She knew she didn't have much time before she suffocated completely. Her body could only heal itself so much.

Tears streamed from her eyes as she squeezed them shut as tightly as she could. She silently counted down from three, and when she hit one, she summoned as much strength as she could. Andie drew her magic inward, and, with one single explosion of release, she propelled it out from her in an effort to free herself from her dirt cage. It worked. The dirt around her exploded in every direction, and she flew up into open air.

She was suddenly and completely free, and she fell to her knees and coughed up dirt and small roots as her panic slowly subsided. She cleared her eyes. She looked back to see her leg and saw that it was so cold because it was bleeding profusely and was probably broken. She looked around her, her heart threatening to explode from her chest. Her eyes streamed and her breath came in ragged gasps.

It was mere moments before her dragonblood began to heal her, though, and the sight of her leg healing calmed her. She rolled over onto her back and tried to look up at the sun. The air was still clouded with dust from the explosion and the sky was completely clouded over. She lay there for a time, healing. When she was feeling better she stood up and took a look around. She couldn't believe her eyes.

She was standing on the side of a mountain. She was on one of the lowest peaks, but there were several others surrounding her and the tallest one was huge. There was no way she was seeing straight. She closed her eyes and opened them again only to find that the mountain was still there and she still wasn't where she was supposed to be. More than that, the sky was completely overcast and green lightning was pounding the earth incessantly in every direction she could see.

Now that she was above ground, the sound was

almost unbearable, like cannons going off over and over and over. Though only the faintest suggestion of the sun came through the thick menacing clouds, the land was alive with the terrible, intermittent flashes of light from the lightning. Wherever the lightning struck, great chunks of land were sent spraying into the air and moderate fires were burning as far as her eyes could see. Far, far below, the earth itself was black and smoldering, completely devoid of any plant life. Lightning ruled the land.

"Well, crap," she swore under her breath. She could barely hear her own voice over the deafening sound of the thunder around her. She tried to process what could have happened, drawing on anything she could possibly muster from her own memory. But it was a fruitless attempt. The last thing she remembered was being on board the ship with her friends. The next, well…

Andie looked around, more frantically this time. "Raesh?" she called, hoping for an answer. "Marvo? Yara? Carmen?" Her calls were met with nothing but a haunting echo as her voice came back to her from the mountainside. When it became clear there was no one else around her, she fell to her knees and held her head in her hands. She opened her mouth and let out a frustrated scream.

But her screams were in vain. There didn't seem to be anyone around to hear her, and even if someone was there, there was no way she could be heard over the weather. She couldn't understand what had happened or why. One minute she was standing in a room with her friends—and her father—the next she was buried alive on the side of the mountain. She closed her eyes and tried to focus.

The last thing she remembered was seeing her father lying in Marvo's bed, looking a great deal weaker than the last time she'd seen him, but smiling up at her. They were finally back together and then they weren't. But no, that wasn't right. She began to remember something. The last thing she'd seen wasn't her father, it was a flash of light. A flash of blue light and blast of cold energy. For a moment she was suspended, then she was buried alive. A spell. That was the only explanation. Someone had spelled her there.

She considered the options. The blue light could have been an attack, and any one of her friends with magic could have sent her away in an effort to protect her. The thought made her smile. Someone must have known or sensed something was going to happen and had been quick on their feet. Quicker than Andie had been, that was for sure. She could barely remember the incident and could easily have been taken out had someone not acted.

"Someone saved me," she said out loud.

But as the words came out of her mouth, she

realized that no one knew where they were headed except for her and the captain. He couldn't have sent her there because he wasn't a sorcerer. Carmen was on the deck with her, but she never went inside the captain's room. There was no one else in the area and the captain wouldn't have had time to upload the coordinates yet.

She then remembered the unfamiliar cold feeling of the magical energy, and knew it hadn't been anyone she recognized. She didn't know the magic she had felt. It was foreign to her.

But then she knew. It had to have been the traitor. But why send her exactly where she wanted to go? Not only that, but they also put her out of reach of themselves and the University. There was nothing to be gained from this. How did they even know where to send her? Maybe they meant to send her somewhere else. None of it made sense.

The only thing she could do for the moment was to try to remember who was in the room. Since she'd woken up in the ground, her mind was completely fuzzy. But she focused and saw it. Yara. Kent. Marvo. Sarinda. Her father. Of course, there was Carmen who came in with her, and Murakami who was standing guard when they arrived. And Lilja, one of the other fighters. Obviously, her father wasn't the traitor. He hadn't even been with them in the tunnels.

But that still left seven people. She wanted to trust

Yara, Carmen, and Marvo outright, but this situation couldn't be taken lightly. If Marvo hadn't trusted Carmen, even for the most obvious reason, then maybe somewhere inside he knew something Andie didn't. After all, Andie hadn't even known Carmen for two years, and Marvo had known her all her life. Murakami had always seemed a bit odd to Andie. And maybe it was a little naive to trust Marvo just because he claimed to have been the first one to recognize that there was a traitor; there was no way to prove that. Even Yara—beautiful, sweet, wise Yara—might not be a true ally. No one had ever really explained why she couldn't be the spy.

What is happening? Andie ran her hands through her hair as she inspected the area surrounding her. It was so foreign, so wild. Thunder crashed overhead as another flash of lightning hit the mountainside not that far behind her. She had to move. It was too dangerous where she was. She could figure out the puzzle of the traitor another time. She couldn't do anything if she was killed by the lightning, anyway.

She stumbled on, not really knowing which direction to take. The lightning pounded the mountainside around her and she was constantly forced to change direction as entire cliffs and stretches of the mountain crumbled around her. She walked and walked and walked, and just when she thought she had made her way substantially down, she realized she'd been going up for the last hour.

But she kept on, looking for something, anything, to help her find her way. Hours passed and so did the day. Time went quickly and although her magic kept her from tiring, Andie grew exhausted in other ways. There didn't seem to be anyone on the face of the planet she could trust, and, worse still, whoever the traitor was, her father was with them. And a ship full of her friends and allies.

One person was about to ruin everything.

CHAPTER EIGHT

JUST WHEN ANDIE WAS ABOUT TO PICK A SPOT TO settle for the night, thinking it was hopeless to try to find her way down with the sun nearly gone, she saw it. A dragon.

It was flying low over the nearest peak, dropping beyond the zenith and coasting along the mountainside. It swooped up and avoided the crags and came soaring across the gulf between that mountain and the one on which Andie stood, propelling itself with more grace in those fleeting seconds than in all the movements Andie had seen in her entire life. She gazed up at it in awe, frozen in place. It seemed to sense when a bolt of lightning was cutting through the air and avoided them with terrific ease. She blinked, her eyes not quite believing what she was seeing. It seemed to be getting bigger. It was coming straight for her.

The dragon flew up and soared until it was at Andie's level and then circled her. It seemed to Andie that the warrior on the dragon's back was looking down and surveying the area. Finally, the dragon landed near her and the warrior bowed from the dragon's back.

"You are Andie," he said, his voice accented with traces of a foreign dialect. He gave her a cautious smile. Andie couldn't help but stare. His hair was long and windblown, the same emerald green as the dragon's hide on which he rode. His eyes shone an even deeper emerald, reflecting the brief flashes of lightning that flickered across the sky above him.

"Yes," she finally managed to say. Her voice was hoarse and she still tasted dirt.

The green-haired man inspected her up and down, a curious look on his face. "Are you well?"

Andie blinked at him, then looked down at the muddy and disheveled state she was in. "I'm... fine," she croaked. She could hardly believe her eyes. "Are you... Are the dragonborn near? Are you all okay?"

She was having trouble wrapping her mind around what was happening to her. Where was she again?

"We're all quite fine," he said, smiling freely now that he was confident who she was. "We've been in these mountains for some time. We've grown happy here. No harm has come to us and we have yet to be spotted, though Saeryn doubts this peace will last."

"Saeryn?" Andie asked, her spirits instantly lifted.

"Yes. She's there with us, of course. Come. I will take you to her."

When the man didn't move, Andie realized what he had just asked her to do. "You mean, on the dragon?"

The warrior's expression looked sly, but he nodded. "Perhaps," he said as he slid gracefully from the dragon's back, landing on two feet next to Andie. He held his hand against the creature's side as he stood gazing at her.

Andie felt numb. She couldn't help but gaze back at the stunning beauty of the man and the dragon, their colors matching in perfect harmony. He wore shimmering armor made from the same scales of his dragon, a brilliant green with jewels and chains and engraved metal—she had never seen anything so stunning in her life. She had of course seen depictions, mostly illustrated texts in books she had secretly found in the University's archives, but seeing the dragon and its rider in person this close, so still, nearly brought a tear to her eye.

The man smiled and took a small step back from his dragon, motioning towards its massive back with one graceful hand. "Try."

Andie did not hesitate. In a world where her

circumstances were constantly changing, where life varied by incredible degrees from moment to moment and where she didn't know who she could trust, the one thing she felt confident of was that these were the people she belonged with. These dragons weren't the evil beasts she grew up hearing about through rumors. She knew better than to trust blindly, but out of everyone she had met and everything she believed in, she knew in her heart that this warrior and his dragon were on her side. She walked over to the dragon, and the dragon turned it's long, scaled neck to look her in the eye. The warrior laughed.

"What's so funny?" Andie asked, turning to face the warrior.

He grinned at the dragon and then bowed his head slightly to Andie. "She says you look like you rolled in dirt."

Andie blinked and couldn't help but stare wide-eyed at him. "She talks?"

"In a way," the man considered. "We riders share a mental connection with our dragons. We understand each other."

"That's... Wow."

The dragon nudged her shoulder with its snout. Andie froze a moment then placed her own hand against its hide. It was not what she expected. She had thought the scales would feel cold, metallic. But they were in fact warm, the scales a smooth silk against her skin. The beast closed her eyes as she touched it, and Andie jumped when she let out a snort.

"She likes you." The warrior grinned, leaning casually against the enormous beast as he watched Andie with a curious look on his face.

Andie smiled at him then turned back to the dragon. "Hello," she finally spoke out loud. She didn't know what else to say. She secretly cursed herself for acting so simple, but her mind was so consumed with wonder and yearning, she didn't even care. All she wanted to do was ride the dragon.

The beast snorted again, small wisps of smoke billowing from its snout. She then knelt on her two front legs, lowering herself for Andie to mount.

"Alright," she said, reaching up to grab hold of the heavy leather harness that wrapped loosely around the dragon's neck. "Here goes nothing."

Andie let out one long deep breath then bent her knees and launched herself up onto the dragon's back. It was by no means a graceful maneuver, but she found her seating, and, when she realized she was actually sitting on a dragon, she couldn't help but let out a long, joyous laugh.

"Interesting," the warrior said, after she'd settled.

Within moments, she was riding a dragon for the first time in her life. She had imagined what it might be like hundreds of times, especially when she was trapped underground for all those months, but she could never have imagined the actual experience.

The dragon lifted from the ground with such power that it left Andie breathless for a moment. She could feel the massive muscles of the dragon's back as it moved beneath her. Its wide, thick wings pumped up and down powerfully and with a sound like two giant, elegant machines of their own.

The iridescence of the dragon's scales shimmered in the flashes of lightning like countless diamonds, and the dragon's entire body was warm and poetic. The head weaved from side to side in front of her. They danced through the lightning and Andie had never felt more exhilarated. It was the most amazing sensation she had ever felt. She closed her eyes and relished in the cool wind that blew her hair as they flew through the skies, an incredible energy coursing through her body like one she'd never experienced.

The warrior rode with a straight back and with the reins in one hand, a true paragon of dignity and patience. Even as the dragon performed swift and daunting maneuvers, he never faltered or gave the slightest suggestion of discomfort. He was totally at ease with the creature.

"Does she have a name?" Andie asked.

"Her name is Ronen," the warrior said. "She is not the fastest or the strongest, but she is the most agile. And she is an even better friend."

As the warrior spoke, the dragon soared up and then allowed itself to fall, soft and graceful even in its descent, until it stretched its wings and cut the air once more. Andie gasped.

"She's showing off," the warrior explained, his voice partially lost in the wind as they soared through the skies. "Not only can we speak to one another mentally, but she can sense my intentions. My emotions. A dragon can read its rider through instinct. Dragons are incredible creatures."

Andie held on tight and marveled for the rest of the journey. For the first time in a very long time, she felt totally and utterly herself. She felt free.

The dragon took them to the tallest peak of the mountain range. Higher and higher they flew, until they cleared the clouds and left the earth and the lightning behind. As soon as they were above the clouds, the sunlight and warmth flooded them, and Andie knew they were in the right place. There were dragons everywhere. Flying, crawling across the side of the mountain, sleeping in groups of several dozen. It seemed there was a dragon in every color imaginable and each was as beautiful as the last and the next.

And moving around among the dragons, Andie could see her people, the dragonborn. They were moving all over the mountain to perform whatever daily tasks needed done. The scene before her took her breath away. She hadn't managed to comprehend just how many had come through the portal that night of the battle at the University. But, seeing them all there, going about their business as if the mountain had been their home for centuries, she couldn't help but marvel in shocked silence.

The warrior brought the dragon down into what looked to be the center of their commerce section, a kind of improvised market square on the mountain side. They had set up the market on one of the level grounds and there must have been three hundred dragonborn there, shopping and enjoying themselves.

When the dragon landed, few people even bothered to take notice of it. They were so use to dragons that one didn't even warrant their notice. But as soon as they noticed that the rider had a passenger with him, they began to stare at Andie and look her over.

"It might be best to give her some space," the warrior said. "She looks like she's already been through a great deal. I'm sure she's just as surprised and thrilled to see all of us as well."

"Who is it," some little kid asked.

"This is Andryne," the warrior said proudly, turning back to Andie. "She is the savior of our people."

"Andie," she corrected, although she wished she hadn't. She would have to get used to her real name now that she was with her own people and didn't have to hide.

Instantly, the clamor began. It was like the people had been waiting for her all their lives. The warrior did his best to hold them back, but one man was not enough. They flocked to Andie. They didn't run up screaming or pulling on her, but they crowded around her and all spoke at once in that calm, graceful way of theirs. They were grateful.

They carefully pushed their wares and baskets out to her, though she declined. It took some time, but the warrior finally extricated himself and Andie from the crowd. He led her back to the mountainside. The people followed. Andie saw that they were approaching a large cavern.

"We have been hard at work making ourselves at home in this new millennium," the warrior said. "Our old mountain no longer exists in the world, but this one will do for now. We have only just begun creating and connecting the caverns. It is slow work, as we do not wish to go too fast or too close together and destabilize the mountain."

"How did you do this?" Andie asked, looking up at the top of the cavern which was easily thirty feet above her.

"Some clever magic and quite a bit of dragon's fire," the warrior said with a grin.

They entered the cavern and walked a

considerable way down into the mountain. Eventually they came to a clearing where fires were lit all around the area and a moderate sized group was meeting in the middle. Standing in the middle of the group was Saeryn. When she saw Andie, she threw up her arms to welcome her. Andie half walked, half ran over and hugged her.

"I'm so relieved," she said, still holding Saeryn. "I was so worried about all of you."

Saeryn was even more regal than Andie remembered. Wearing a flowing lilac dress with slits along the leg for easy movement, and magenta dragonscale and intricately-woven metallic armor and crown, she looked like a vision of fantasy. Her strong arms held Andie tight, the glistening scales reflecting the warm light of the surrounding fires. The armor was mesmerizing. Everything about the woman was mesmerizing.

"We're just fine," Saeryn said, beaming. "Though we were just as worried about you. How have you come? Where are your friends?"

"I don't know. One minute I was with all of them on a ship and the next I was buried alive on the side of this mountain."

Gasps went through the crowd as they all stood in shock and awe. Andie looked out at the surrounding dragonborn, her heart suddenly full. Her people surrounded her, gazing upon her with curiosity and kindness. She couldn't help but smile out at them as she took in the scene before her.

Warriors, workers, and children alike were gathered around the fires, dragons dozing peacefully around them. Andie noticed the men and women clad in various forms of dragonscale armor stood near their dragons, all of which reflected the same colors as their riders.

Blues, greens, golds, and reds glistened in the firelight, each unique set of armor different and more beautiful from the next. The eyes and hair of each rider the same matching hues as their dragon counterparts. Andie had never seen such a display. It filled her with such wonder. She had so much to learn about her people.

"Who did that to you?" the warrior demanded, his hand on his sword. Andie's attention was drawn back to the green-scaled warrior.

"I don't know. I was surrounded by my friends and then there was this flash of blue light and an incredibly powerful burst of cold energy. And then I was underground. I don't know exactly what happened, but someone in that room cast a spell on me. The day before, I had just found out that we had a traitor onboard. Someone had been spying on us for the University, but I never learned who."

"They're cleverer than I thought," Saeryn said, her eyes narrowing with great concern. "But that is a matter for another time. Has your dragonblood healed you?"

"Yes."

"Good. How long ago was it that you saw your friends?"

"Earlier today. This morning."

"Did anything happen in the time you were on the ship?"

"No, nothing I can remember. We hid under ground for two hundred and forty days, beneath the University. We came up on the one hundred and ninety-first day of this year. That was two days ago. Since then—"

"The one hundred and ninety-first day?" Saeryn interrupted. "But that would make this the one hundred and ninety-third."

"Right. So, then we were at sea and—"

"But that's impossible," Saeryn insisted, with a look on her face that Andie couldn't understand.

"What do you mean 'impossible?'"

"Today is the two hundred and twenty-sixth day of the year."

Andie stared at Saeryn. That couldn't be. It was the same day, it had to be.

"No, that's not right," Andie said. "We boarded on 191 and this morning was 193."

"I'm sorry, but it's not. We've kept excellent track of our passage in this world and made every effort to stay appraised of the world's ways. Today is 226."

"But that means that... I've been... away... for thirty-three days. But how?"

"Your back," Saeryn said, suddenly overcome with nervous energy. "Let me see your back."

"Does she have the marks?" the warrior asked.

Andie turned around and allowed Saeryn to check her back. She heard more gasps from the people nearby and turned back to Saeryn. Andie began to feel her own back in a kind of mute and frantic terror.

"What's wrong with me?" she asked. "What's back there? What have they done to me?"

"This," Saeryn said, turning to show Andie her back.

Andie could see that Saeryn had a blue tattoo on her back, only more like a scar than something done on purpose. It looked like a hurried infinity symbol with a harsh L drawn in the exact center. The entire design was glowing blue. Saeryn turned around to face Andie again.

"Eitilt," she said. "The time curse."

"What?" Andie said, still feeling her back.

"We know it well. It was the spell the sorcerers used to trap our people. That spell was older, more powerful, and it stretched from the day they overpowered us to the day you freed us. Centuries. It would appear that the one that was cast on you was more hurried, narrower, but the result is the same. You were taken from your time and put down in the future. In this case—"

"Thirty-three days," Andie said, dumbfounded. "I can't believe this. What about my friends? Are they okay? Are they even alive?"

"I don't know. I'm so sorry, my dear Andryne."

"I believe she goes by Andie," the warrior mentioned as he strode past. He winked at her as she caught his eye.

Just then a powerful bolt of lightning stabbed the mountain and shook the cavern so hard that stalactites fell from the ceiling. Saeryn disintegrated them with a wave of her hand, including one that fell directly over Andie.

"What is this place?" Andie asked. "Where are we?"

"These lands were known by another name in our time, but I believe your era calls this the Hot Salts of Mithraldia."

"So, I was right. You came here to throw the University off your trail."

"Not merely the University, but the world. Andie, why didn't you protect yourself? You could have used magic to destroy that falling thing."

"I can't use magic. I still have my icon. It's a kind of monitoring device that all the students at the University have to wear in order to attend. We haven't been able to do magic since the night of the portal because the University can track us if we do and..."

Andie's hands flew to her head. She couldn't believe she'd been so stupid.

"No! I used my magic to pull myself out of the ground. The University will have noticed that. I'm so sorry, Saeryn. I don't know how I could have been so careless."

Saeryn moved forward and took Andie by her shoulders. She smiled down at her and just the expression on her face brought Andie to a calmer state.

"Andie, it's fine. We've covered these peaks with protective magic. And if by some chance they did monitor your actions and decided to come here, they would not find themselves very welcome. After the carnage of their last battle with us, I do not believe they would be so eager to attack again, not without some weapon or magic much more powerful than what they possessed last time. However, if there is a traitor among your company and if that traitor did indeed send you here, then the University already knows where to come for you. And us. But none of that is your fault, nor should it be your concern. You did an ineffable service to us in bringing us out of that portal. We know you would never willingly compromise us. It is not your fault that there is evil in the world."

Andie felt much better after Saeryn's words and she took a few deep breaths to calm herself. She looked around the group and everyone was smiling at her. No one was angry or concerned. She truly was among her own kind. As she looked at the faces, she saw one she remembered. Lymir. When he saw that she was looking at him, he came over to her. She hugged him.

"It does me a world o' good to see ye, girl," he said, holding her tight. "I hadn't been sure I would. Tell me, ye still carry the ole bracelet I give ye?"

"I haven't taken it off yet," she said, holding up her wrist. "But I'm confused. What are you doing here?"

"All in proper time," he said, smiling and turning to Saeryn.

"Andie, did anyone else on your ship know where you wanted to come?"

"Yes. The captain."

"And can he be trusted?"

"He'll follow the heading, of that I'm sure. But if you want the truth, Saeryn, I don't know if anyone on that ship can be trusted."

"Very well. If you were taken thirty-three days ago then they should be getting close to us by now, no doubt coming from the sea down the long belly of the Nathair River that runs behind the mountain. For now, we'll get that thing out of you. We have no surgeons, as dragonblood heals us, but there are those of us who are skilled in medicinal magic. We should have you free of the University's eye within the hour."

Saeryn had not lied. In a little less than an hour, the chief examiner of the dragonborn, Gordenson, had removed the icon from Andie. The process was slow and painful, and eventually revealed yet another deception of the University. The icon, once inserted into the palm, began to slowly burrow its way deeper into the host with each passing day. Eventually it settled up somewhere around the heart; it only appeared to stay in the palm because it was spelled to manifest its light and sensations there. Gordenson said that with time the University probably would have been able to kill the host with a mere whisper of a spell—an unbelievably deadly prediction seeing as to how more than a third of the sorcerers in Noelle were educated at the University and they all kept the icons for life. Gordenson finally removed Andie's through her back.

CHAPTER NINE

FOR THE NEXT THREE DAYS, ANDIE LIVED AMONG HER people and began to learn their ways. She began to learn their language and customs, how they prepared their food and what life was like in the time from which they came. She learned a lot about the dragons, too, including what to feed them and how each dragonborn could develop an extrasensory relationship with their dragon. She never allowed herself to grow content or to forget the circumstances that she could never run from, but she was aware that she was dangerously close to being fulfilled.

However, countless things still weighed heavily on her. She couldn't stop wondering who the traitor was or if the rest of her friends had figured it out. She was worried about her father; she'd only seen him for a few seconds, but even then he looked weak, tired. And if there was someone onboard strong enough to cast a spell on her and land her in the future, then she had no idea what else that person might be capable of. She had finally calmed down enough to think rationally, however. She knew Marvo couldn't be the traitor because he had no magic; she'd been so shaken and startled before that she hadn't even considered it. Her father was out. But that still left six people.

She was willing to give Carmen and Yara the benefit of the doubt after some thought, possibly even Murakami. Though, Andie wouldn't fully pull them off the list, she was so jarred by it all. She knew very little about Kent, Sarinda, and Lilja and at first that was enough for her to convict them. But the issue with that theory was that those three were essentially small cogs in the machine of the rebellion. Andie couldn't think of a single instance where those three had been included in major decision-making or had been privy to anything but the most obvious plans. How could they spy if they didn't have access to the pertinent information? Access that Carmen, Yara, and Murakami had plenty of. It was hopeless.

At least with her icon removed Andie could enjoy her magic again. She took advantage of the seclusion of the mountain and the knowledge of Saeryn and began to practice and to increase her power. Even Saeryn was impressed. Andie made many new friends among her people, most notably the warrior who'd picked her up when she first arrived. His name was Oren and he seemed to have taken an instant liking to Andie. He never crowded her, but always made himself available to her and was kinder and more attentive than anyone else. Andie greatly admired him and they spent a lot of time sharing stores about their vastly different lives.

On the morning of Andie's fifth day on the mountain, the two hundred and thirtieth day of the year, a ship was spotted on the Nathair. Oren saw it while out on watch duty and reported it to Saeryn. From the description he gave, Andie knew it was her ship. She was happy and devastated that they had finally arrived: she had no idea what to expect. For all she knew the traitor had taken over the ship and allowed the University professors and Searchers to board. Or maybe it was just the traitor and everyone onboard was dead. Or maybe the traitor had been discovered and contained, and everything was alright. She honestly had no idea what was coming up that river for her.

Saeryn suggested that a party be formed to meet the travelers at the ship, rather than allow the unidentified traitor to see their actual caverns. Oren, Saeryn, and a few others mounted dragons and pushed off from the mountainside to plunge down to the earth. Andie rode with Oren.

The dragons dove in perfect lines, curving only

just enough to avoid touching the mountain. They met and cut through the black clouds and suddenly Andie found herself among the fierce lightning again. The sound was incredible, the vibrations and energy of the air were bracing. The dragons dove as if there was nothing in the world that could hurt them. They soared down, down, down, until they were mere yards above the river and then they leveled out and flew straight for the ship.

As they came closer, Andie could see that there were no people on the decks of the ship. Everybody was below deck, maybe because of the lightning. Andie couldn't tell. The riders made their dragons fly a brief circle around the ship for reconnaissance and then Oren and Saeryn landed on the upper deck. The weight of the two dragons rocked the ship and the deck groaned under their bulk. The other warriors decided to fly high and nearby to keep a watch over the ship and its surroundings. They flew up into the thunderous sky. Andie, Saeryn, and Oren dismounted and Andie led them toward the captain's room, but before they rounded the corner, they were met by two people. The captain and Raesh.

Before Andie could register that it was real or could get a word out, Raesh had her in his arms. She didn't know how long they stayed like that. She realized then that she hadn't known how badly, how deeply, she had missed him. And now that she knew for certain that he wasn't the traitor—he hadn't been anywhere near that room—it made the reunion that much sweeter. They finally let each other go, but couldn't stop smiling.

"What happened to you? Where have you been?" Raesh began. "How did you get here? How long have you been here? Are you hurt? Are your people okay? Did you—"

"I'm fine, Raesh," she said with a smile, grabbing his arms to calm him. "Everything is fine. Someone who was in the room with me cast a spell and sent me to the future. I landed on the mountainside five days ago and I've been with my people ever since. They're all fine. What about you? What happened after I was gone?"

"Chaos. When you disappeared, everything went into anarchy. Factions formed, suspicions grew, everyone was scared and confused. We almost had a civil war. No one could figure out what happened to you. We put everyone who was in the room with you in individual cells and spelled them so that they couldn't talk to anyone, including each other."

"What about your father?"

"Him, too. I know he doesn't have magic, but that doesn't mean he couldn't have been in on it somehow."

"Raesh, you can't be serious."

"Andie, I wouldn't have thought anyone in that

room would ever want to hurt you, let alone be powerful enough to make you disappear. I love him, but I had to."

"A sacrifice I'm sure he understands," said Saeryn.

"I'm sorry. Raesh, you remember Saeryn from the portal. She's the Queen of my people. And this is Oren, one of the dragonborn warriors. Oren, Saeryn, this is Raesh and the captain."

Everyone exchanged greetings pleasantly, though Andie did not miss a certain hesitancy between Raesh and Oren. The captain led them back to the control room.

"It wasn't easy getting here," he said. "Coming from the sea to the mouth of the Nathair brought us through the Gray Fold."

"Yes, we know of that," Saeryn said. "Even in our time many ship would take a longer route than risk going through those turbulent waters. Most who attempted it did not return."

"We almost went around ourselves, but time was of the essence. Luckily for us, ships are a lot stronger these days. There was some contention about which mountain range to take, but I finally broke and told Raesh that you had picked this one, Andie, and so on we came."

"There's been contention about everything," Raesh said, his hands on his hips. "We're barely holding it together, but seeing you and your people is going to do everybody a lot of good, Andie. Everybody calmed down some when it was decided that the traitor had to have been someone in that room, though we still had no idea what happened. Narrowing it down to eight people out of five hundred helped. But you're what we need."

"I'll meet with them," Andie said. "But until we figure out exactly what happened and who did it, it's probably best that everyone stays on the ship. For the protection of my people."

"We should go down now and let you bring peace," Saeryn said. "Oren, wait here with the captain and we will try to be brief."

Oren bowed and took up a post near the map. Andie smiled at him, but he only barely returned it. Raesh led them out and then down to the lower decks where Andie began to listen for sounds of the passengers, but there was nothing. It was silent. They went down another level to where the cabins were and even there it was eerily quiet. Even Saeryn seemed ill at ease in the halls. Eventually they came to the large meeting room where the fighters had been meeting the day Andie disappeared. It was totally empty. The three of them walked in and up to the platform.

"We can wait here," said Raesh. "They should be coming in soon. The captain made the announcement to meet here when we saw the dragons approaching."

"What's taking them so long?" Andie asked.

"They didn't want to come until they were armed and ready to fight. I'm sorry, Andie, but we didn't know that you were here and we didn't know if your people would be friendly with us after we told them we'd lost you."

"A sound judgement," Saeryn said. "We would not have attacked you and we would have welcomed you with open arms, but it would have undone a great amount of trust to have come without our savior."

Andie cringed at the word—it didn't seem fitting. She'd gotten them out of the portal, but that hardly counted for saving them. As soon as they were out, the dragonborn had to save her and her friends from being wiped out by the University. Moreover, the dragonborn had been forced to go out on their own and face the new world, and Andie hadn't been any help to them. They had saved her again on the mountainside.

"This is spinning out of control," Andie said. "We're supposed to be fighting the University, not each other. I can't believe one person could do this to us. Are you any closer to figuring out who the spy is?"

"If anything, we're starting to backtrack," Raesh said. "This morning one of the factions started talking about how the spell might have been cast from outside the room, meaning we're right back to having everyone on the suspect list. I don't know how we're going to do it, but we need to devise a plan to smoke this person out."

As Raesh finished, the fighters began to stream in. Those of them that were humans came in covered with ammunition and holding their weapons of choice. Those of them who were sorcerers kept their hands slightly clinched, ready to cast at a moment's notice. From the way they regarded one another as they came in Andie couldn't tell if they were more threatened by what the dragonborn might do or by each other.

They came in, cautious, and came down to the front looking as if they or the situation might explode at any moment. But then they saw Andie and the change came over them: pure relief. They came up to her and shook her hand or hugged her and asked her so many questions at once that she couldn't make any of them out. They didn't quite allow themselves to smile, but the whole room seemed to take on a new atmosphere when their eyes met her face. She could tell then, for the first time, just how scared they truly were.

More and more fighters piled into the room and the crowd rotated so that the newcomers could all see Andie and see that she was alright. Andie tried to give them as much hope and reassurance as she could. When everyone was finally present and accounted for, Raesh called the meeting to order.

"Alright, everybody," Raesh began. "For anyone

who doesn't know yet, Andie is alive, she's fine, and she's back here with us now. She's found her people and they're on our side. Their Queen, Saeryn, is here with us tonight. Let's pay her our respect."

With his words, every fighter in the room bowed to the Queen. Raesh bowed, too. The Queen acknowledged them with a deft nod of her head.

"I'm glad we could all set aside our fears long enough to gather in the same room," Raesh continued. "And I know it's going to be a long, hard road back to trusting each other, but I think it starts here, today, with Andie."

Raesh turned to Andie and gestured for her to step forward and address the crowd, which she wasn't expecting. Andie moved to the front of the platform and looked out at the crowd. Most of those faces she didn't even know; most of the people she had never even talked to. But she understood that at that moment they needed her.

"I won't talk long because Saeryn has several things to tell you, but I want you to know that the true enemy is the University. Not us. Not each other. While it is true that there is a traitor onboard, I want you to know that I was in that room and the spell had to have come from someone who was in there with me. That means one of the eight people you have locked up is the spy. Everyone in this room can be trusted."

"What if there's more than one spy?" someone

called out. "What happens if only one of them is in a cell?"

"What happens if the ship sinks?" Andie countered. "What happens if the lightning strikes the ship and fries the navigation system? What happens if the sky falls down? We can't afford to worry about problems we don't know we have. What we do know is that one person aboard this ship is a traitor. What we also know is that more than five hundred people onboard this ship are true allies. Which of those facts do you want to focus on?"

She paused for a minute to let the words sink in and the crowd seemed to think on it hard, as if they'd never considered it.

"I'm happy to be back with you and I'm still eternally grateful that you're all here willing to risk your lives for my people and me. But if we can't trust each other then we're dead already. We need to rebuild this unit or the fight will not go our way. And don't put all of your hope into me. Have faith in yourselves. I do."

CHAPTER TEN

Andie backed up, not wanting to push her luck with her crowd. She knew her presence was helping, but her followers had been through so much in the past few weeks that she didn't want to risk pushing them too far too fast. Instead, Saeryn stepped up to the front and her presence there was awe-inspiring, such grace and strength and peace.

"I would be remiss and shameful if I didn't first thank you for the sacrifices you've made in order to be here, fighting for my people. None of you are dragonborn and none of you have any obligation to us, and yet you've given up your comfort and potentially your lives in order that we might live. It is not a debt we can ever repay, but if you have need of us we will come without hesitation. I thank you on behalf of myself and my people.

"I don't know how familiar you are with the story of the dragonborn, so perhaps a brief recapitulation might be in order. We are a people out of time; we come from an era centuries ago, when the war between the sorcerers and the dragonborn was at its culmination. We fled to a safe haven in the mountains and Andie saved us by pulling us through the portal and across time, saving us by allowing us to take advantage of the very spell the University used to try to annihilate us. That is how we've come to your modern time. Very few were on our side back then, but there were some who fought for us. One in particular was a sorcerer who went to battle with us time and time again. He came through the portal alone some years ago. His name is Lymir."

At those words, Andie found herself almost breathless. She didn't know if she couldn't believe that Lymir was from ancient times or that he didn't tell her. It explained so much about his knowledge and the way he had looked out for her. It explained how he knew so much about the portal. Saeryn turned to Andie.

"The bracelet he gave you was to ensure that you didn't fall through the portal when you pulled us out. Lymir well knew the power of that door. It's quite a long fall from being a powerful sorcerer to running a tavern with questionable clientele, but do not underestimate him. We all owe him a great debt."

Andie could hardly believe her ears. She fidgeted with the bracelet on her wrist, realizing how much sense Saeryn's words actually made. She always wondered about the tavern keeper and how he knew so much about everything.

"Lymir was once head of your Council," Saeryn continued, addressing the crowd again. "In fact, he was the one who conceived it all those centuries ago. He was also the appointed instructor of a royal line of sorcerers during that time, a position which afforded him great access and influence. He joined our cause after that line began to commit crimes against my people out of fear and envy. That was when the entire world decided it no longer wanted to live with us. But I assure you, we are a peaceful race. Our dragons may be fierce and our magic may be formidable, but we have always abhorred conflict. We are a simple people with simple desires. The hate against us that persists in your time began in ours. The sorcerers wanted us gone so that they could command Noelle unopposed. They knew that despite our kind ways, we would never let them subjugate a single city, let alone the entire land. Just as ourselves when we came through the portal, Lymir was heartbroken when he arrived in your time and found that the sorcerers had not only won, but that the people didn't even realize what had happened. How they had been deceived and brought down. He lived among you disheartened, having only one piece remaining to him of the time he knew. That piece was the bracelet that he gave to Andie to protect her. In fact, that bracelet once belonged to me."

Saeryn looked at Andie with a smile. Andie suddenly felt extremely guilty, almost as if she had stolen the bracelet from Saeryn by force. Without even thinking, Andie began to take the bracelet off and give it to the Queen, but Saeryn held up her hand to stop her.

"Keep that, savior," Saeryn said, never losing her smile. "If it weren't for that bracelet, you might not have survived pulling our people through that portal. Only the strongest of us could have succeeded in that task, and only you could have succeeded in such a feat. Lymir would not have chosen you for nothing. He saw in you what I see in you. Our future.

Andie stared down at her feet, considering. Her fingers played with the bracelet as she listened.

"I feel I've spoken enough now. I just want you all to understand that this fight is an old one and is sure to grow ugly before its end. My people and I are at your service and rest assured, we will not leave you to fight our battles by yourselves. But I implore you to trust each other. Raesh and Andie have assured me that the traitor is indeed one of the people you've captured downstairs. They cannot hurt you from a cell. Be at peace and be together. The enemy is out there, not in here. Thank you."

It was quieter than ever when Saeryn finished. No one clapped or moved. They barely breathed. Andie never knew so many people gathered in one place could be so quiet. She could tell that they had been lifted, inspired, relieved, but they were so in awe of Saeryn—and of Andie, too—that they didn't seem to know what the proper response was. Saeryn descended the platform and went out into the hall. Andie and Raesh followed, leaving the fighters to conduct themselves.

"I'm so grateful for this," Andie said, indicating her bracelet. "It means the world to me."

"As it once did to me," said Saeryn. "It suits you."

"I've been thinking... I was thinking about all the things you told me about the dragons and the dragonborn. How all dragonborn people are born with a link to a dragon. How the scale patterns on our skin are a symbol of our dragon until we are united with them. I was just wondering if, perhaps somewhere, there was a dragon out there for me?"

"I'm afraid I do not have the answer to that. We have lost so many of the amazing creatures over the past centuries at the hands of the sorcerers. We once lived in peace and all dragonborn had a companion, but now only few remain and not even all warriors have a dragon bonded to them anymore. I do not believe there is a dragon living who is to be bonded with you. At least, not until the dragons begin to mate again and new dragons are born. When the sorcerers began their hunt for the dragons, long before my time, our people grew weaker. In turn, as our people were massacred, the dragons themselves grew sparse. They stopped reproducing, our people began to grow weaker, which is how the sorcerers first began to overcome us."

"Well, I have the scales," Andie said, hesitant. "What does that mean?"

"It means that perhaps someday a dragon will be born to you, but until then I'm afraid you will never be able to reach your full potential."

"I see." Andie tried to shrug it off, but she knew it was obvious how disappointed she was. "Saeryn, may I ask one more question? It's a difficult one to ask."

Saeryn smiled and placed her hand on Andie's shoulder. "You may ask me anything, always."

Andie paused for a moment to collect her thoughts. "Oren has green hair and green eyes. His dragon is the same color. I noticed all the warriors and their bonded dragons are of the same coloring."

Saeryn nodded. "Yes, it is a sign of their bond. A dragon is destined to pair with one unique dragonborn, and one only. From birth, the dragons already demonstrate the same coloring as its soul partner."

Andie wasn't sure how to ask her question without hurting the Queen. Her friend. Finally, she let out a deep breath and just asked. "I couldn't help but notice your dragon is of a different color."

A long moment passed in silence and Saeryn hung her head in mourning. "Oriander, my dragon… Ori. He didn't make it through the portal when you pulled us through. He sacrificed himself to protect our people when that evil spell was cast. He hung back to ensure we all made it through the portal safely, but I'm afraid it closed before he was able to follow. He was a great dragon, and an even greater companion."

Sorrow struck Andie's heart at those words. "I'm… I'm so sorry, Saeryn. Had I known, I…"

"There was nothing you could do, sweet girl," Saeryn smiled. "You saved our people, and for that I owe you a great debt. You are our savior, and never forget that."

"Then who's dragon do you ride now?"

"My dearest friend, one I considered a sister, did not survive that final attack from the sorcerers. Raylim, her dragon, came through the portal just as she fell. Normally, a dragon would not survive the death of its rider, but I summoned all my strength to keep him alive. He bonded to me, in a way. We have become close, growing stronger from each other's presence, although it will never be the same bond that Ori and I shared. Or that Raylim and Katyara shared. Nevertheless, we endure. And I am eternally grateful for the strength and companionship he offers me."

Andie couldn't bear the sorrow in Saeryn's eyes, but she straightened her back and offered a smile to the Queen as best she could. "I am so sorry for your loss. Raylim is lucky to have you."

"And I him," Saeryn answered.

Raesh rounded the corner and came to stand next to Andie. He opened his mouth to speak, but quickly shut it as he recognized the emotion that hung in the air.

When Andie looked back down to her feet, Saeryn lifted her chin with a gentle finger. "I know this disappoints you, Andie. Not having a dragon of your own. But this is a different time, and perhaps someday, when things are different, you will find your match. But, right now, we must focus on stopping the spread of hate and malice. We need to convince the world that the dragonborn are actually good. That we aren't the monsters the University has purported us to be. You know as well as I that the University is in the midst of creating something terrible. I suppose now we should go down."

Andie took in a deep breath and let it out slowly. Saeryn was right, of course. She shouldn't let the fact that she doesn't have a dragon of her own impede her mission. She had never grown up even considering it an option, so why should it bother her now?

Saeryn turned to Raesh. "I understand that Andie's father is down there as well?"

113

"Yes," Raesh nodded, wrapping his arm around Andie's shoulder. He always knew what to do and what to say. "We put him down there, but only to sort of save face. People were so on edge that they wanted all of them locked up, even though Eric had only joined us onboard and couldn't possibly be the spy. I'm sorry, Andie. But I've made him as comfortable as possible and made sure he was treated with respect from the beginning."

"It's okay, Raesh, I understand," Andie said, genuinely not angry. "Let's go down."

It was a short walk down to the brig. The place was clean and quiet, but there were thirty guards stationed around the room. They seemed highly on edge, though they all calmed considerably when they saw that Andie was alive and well. They came to the first of the cells.

"They start here," Raesh said. "On this end are the three fighters. First Kent, then Lilja, then Sarinda."

Kent was very amiable. He didn't seem upset at all, as if it all made sense to him.

"I'm glad you're okay," he said. "With Marvo locked up I know it must have been hard on Raesh organizing everyone and trying to keep the peace. Even before we knew there was a traitor it was hard to keep us all in check. We come from different backgrounds and cities. Some of them hate each other as much as they hate the University. The only thing that holds us together is the will to do what's right."

"You seem like a really sweet guy, Kent," Andie said. "If you're not the one who betrayed us, then I'm truly sorry."

"Don't be. I understand. The needs of the many outweigh one guy's kindness. I know you're doing what you have to do. Stay strong."

Andie stopped at each of the cells, but Sarinda and Lilja refused to talk to her and barely even looked in her direction. They did, however, show deference to Saeryn before going back into their reticent modes.

They came to Murakami next. She wasn't as belligerent as Sarinda or as cold as Lilja, but she was also the same woman she'd always been—terse. She didn't hold much conversation, though she was interested in what Saeryn had to say about the ancient relationships of the Raeynese empire. After her, they came to Andie's father, and, even though it was against protocol, Raesh opened the door and let her in to see him.

"Oh, I'm so glad to see you," she said. "I was so worried something might happen to you."

"I'm fine," Eric said. "I've been out of my mind worrying about you. You just disappeared. I didn't know where or how or why. Oh, my beautiful girl. Your mother would be so proud of you."

"Dad, are you sure you're okay? Can I get you anything?"

"Andie, I'm fine. Traveling at sea is a little rougher than I expected, but I'm completely—"

"Dad, I'm so sorry I stopped calling as often and that I didn't come home the last time we planned. I'm sorry I couldn't control my magic and avoid ever going to the University in the first place. I'm sorry I haven't been here to protect you and that I've been so selfish and careless and—"

"Andie, stop. I have never been more proud of you. I never doubted that you loved me for a second and I knew how much you needed to go to the University, and not just for your abilities. For answers. Honey, you're going to mean a lot of things to a lot of people, but you're also going to be the savior of your race. I know you can do it. Your mother knew it, too. Don't ever worry about me. Go and save the world."

"She has already made a fine start," said Saeryn, going down before Eric as he lay in the bed. "I am Saeryn, Queen of the dragonborn, and I want you to know that your daughter is more than we had ever dreamed. I regret so much that your wife cannot be here to witness the courage and the strength of your incredible daughter. I thank you for lending her to us."

"It is my pleasure. Thank you for welcoming her into her people. She's needed it her entire life."

They stayed with Eric for a long while, but eventually moved on. Marvo was sleeping, but even when they woke him, he seemed devoid of life. He was grateful that Andie was okay and that she'd found her people, but beyond that he seemed totally drained of the vitality that he had possessed the last time Andie saw him. Raesh turned to her after they moved on.

"Something happened to him when you disappeared," Raesh said. "It was like the traitor suddenly became... real. I think all that time he was hoping that he was wrong, that there was no traitor or that the person would truly come over to our side. But when whoever it was spelled you out my dad just... withered. I think he lost his faith in all of us, in all of this."

Carmen was beside herself.

"Are you freaking kidding me! The future? That's both cool and disturbing. Are you okay? How are you getting along with your people?"

"Everything and everyone is great, Carmen. I'm glad you're okay, too."

"Are you, Andie? I can tell from the way you're looking at me that you don't see me as the same girl you used to know. I can't imagine how all of this must make you feel. I know it must have seriously shaken your faith in people and in everything we're fighting for, but believe me when I tell you that I am *not* the traitor. Do you remember that story that I told you back in the tunnels?"

"Yeah, I remember."

"That's me. That's who I am. I'm not perfect and I'm not always kind, but I would die before I betrayed you or anything important to you. Remember that."

Finally, there was Yara. When Raesh waved his hand to clear the visibility between them, Yara jumped to her feet, but then she froze. Andie didn't know what the movement meant. Yara had a look on her face that Andie had never seen before. Andie didn't realize it, but she was standing just as still as Yara, with an expression just as confusing.

"Andie?"

Yara's voice sounded more like a little girl's. She almost looked as if she didn't know where she was or what was happening. Andie wanted to say something, but couldn't. She didn't know how she felt to see Yara again. She wasn't even sure if she knew who the girl in front of her was. Everything Andie had believed about the people in those cells had been turned on its head, with the exception of her father.

"Perhaps we should give them some time alone," Saeryn said.

Raesh nodded and the two of them walked off around the corner. Raesh cleared the guards on the hallway. Andie and Yara were left alone.

CHAPTER ELEVEN

"I WANT TO THANK YOU ALL FOR COMING IN TODAY. I'm sure there must be a plethora of other duties you need to attend to. Legislation, public relations, the fortification of your individual cities and regions. Thank you for taking time out of your busy schedules."

"None of us are here to endure your false gratitude, Myamar. This polite request for a meeting is only farce. It's you trying to mask your ego under a guise of friendship."

"Stefan, your verbal contributions are, as always, endearing, but—"

"Of all the people in the world, Myamar, I'm the last one you want to condescend to."

Chancellor Mharú went silent for a moment. Everyone knew that he hated Stefan with a passion, but was too incompetent and frightened of him to do anything. Stefan was very old and very powerful. When the terrorist attacks began in Taline all those years ago, it was Stefan who almost singlehandedly brought the city back to its feet and he who had been unanimously declared protector of the city. Stefan had been in a number of dangerous and legendary battles throughout the history of western Noelle—battles that stretched back at least one hundred fifty years. No one was really sure who he was or what he was capable of, but there was not a sorcerer in all of Noelle who would ever risk fighting with him. Not to mention Chancellor Mharú was, and had always been, a coward.

"Moving on," he said, turning his eyes from Stefan. "The abominations known as the dragonborn have eluded us for the time being. But I'm confident that we will find them soon and when we do I—"

"You won't find them, Myamar," Stefan said. "These people are an ancient, powerful race. The time may be different and the land may have changed, but their power hasn't. If they don't want to be found, then they won't be. Don't you have other things to focus on besides continuing this futile campaign of hate?"

"What's important is that the people feel safe and they won't be able to do that until every last one of the dragonborn and their dragons have been hunted down and exterminated."

"Okay, Myamar. Have your little hunt. Scour the ends of Noelle and the seas looking for the ancient, powerful, self-healing race who ride giant fire-breathing creatures whose claws could shred you with a single swipe. Spend all of that exorbitant tax you levied on the region in order to fund a journey that will yield nothing. Ignore the University that has been ruined in body and reputation. Strain what few political connections you have left. But you know what, I wish you the best of luck. I hope you find them. And when your mother comes to me, begging me to go and bring you home, I'm going to hand over to her the charred remains of your body. And I'm going to laugh."

With that Stefan stood and began to leave. The other dignitaries, chancellors, mayors, and politicians began to whisper nervously. Stefan was by far the most powerful among them and they desperately wanted him in their fight against the dragonborn. One of them stood and addressed him.

"Stefan, please," she said. "We need you to get behind this. Many of us only came because we assumed you would be as eager to hunt down these... monsters as Chancellor Mharú. Won't you fight for your people? Won't you represent the city of Taline in this great battle?"

Stefan stopped halfway out of the door. He was still for a moment and then he turned slowly, his eyes terribly focused.

"I fight for my people every day. You don't know what it's like to wake up and not know if your city is still going to be there when the sun goes down. Every day I watch and I wait and I fear for every soul in that city. Not a single year has gone by in the last two decades when we haven't had at least a handful of attacks. Bombings. Poisonings. Mass hexes. And you think I'm going to turn my back on them to help you hunt down innocent people who just want to live life after *your* ancestors tried to deny it to them? The dragonborn aren't abominations. They're people. They frighten you because they're more powerful than you, yet you're the ones itching to fight. Your narrowmindedness is unbelievable. I'm going home to look over my people. Do yourselves a favor and let this go. Otherwise... you're all dead."

Stefan left the room and there was a deep and wide silence for a while. Even Chancellor Mharú couldn't get up the stomach to talk for a few moments. He knew that they were all reconsidering backing his ploy. It was different when they believed they were going to have Stefan behind them, but now they were being led by a coward whose only claims to prestige and power came from a family name that he wasn't smart enough to know he needed.

Fortunately, they all possessed some idea of loyalty and wanted, at the very least, to see the thing through.

"Well, we all know how paranoid and close-minded Stefan can sometimes be," Chancellor Mharú began. "It doesn't change the fact that we need to find them, kill them, and take back Noelle."

"How?" asked one of the dignitaries. "I've spoken with some of the professors who were here that night and fought the dragonborn. They say the power of those people is unlimited, that they can heal themselves and fight like raging warriors. How do we defend against that?"

"How many of us will die in the fighting and never get to enjoy the freedom we fought so hard for?" another asked. "People need assurances."

"What can we honestly do about these people and their power?"

"Your eyes are on the wrong future," the chancellor said, looking more devious than they had ever seen.

Chancellor Mharú came down from the podium and walked over to the side of the room. All the people in the meeting turned in their chairs to follow him with their eyes. The Chancellor stopped in the middle of the space and clapped his hands. A door materialized in the wall and as it slid up silver beings moved into the room and stood stock still. They made no noise and the members of the gathering instinctively leaned away from them.

"Ladies and gentlemen, I give you the Sentinels," the chancellor said proudly. "Perhaps you've heard of them? Most of us were told bedtime stories as children about the incredibly power beings who worked for peace in the Old World. These are the original thirteen who worked so tirelessly to maintain order in the ancient days of Noelle. These beings are centuries old, dating back to at least the time of Hightowyr, maybe earlier. They are notoriously difficult to kill. So difficult, in fact, that in all these long centuries no one has been able to kill a single one."

"But I thought three of them were destroyed when the criminals escaped from the University?" someone asked.

"No, merely damaged. The best part is that the Sentinels were instrumental in taking down the dragonborn centuries ago and I have no doubt that they can be just as helpful today. And do you know what else?"

The members of the meeting were interested now, had forgotten the chancellor's poor history and were growing more and more intrigued by his current machinations. Some of them were even beginning to hope.

"To this day, Sentinels are the only beings in the history of the world to be able to kill dragons."

The joyous gasps rang throughout the assembly and the members began to smile, to clap, and even to nod their approval to Chancellor Mharú. The chancellor himself began to feel his pride swell again. He was no fool, he knew how badly he had sullied the family name and how far he had to go to regain his reputation and influence. The defeat in the Archives at the hands of the dragonborn had been a devastating blow to his political career. He was desperate, but he was clever.

"And if that's not enough..."

The chancellor clapped his hands again and seconds later, a man came out dressed in all black—a black purer and deeper than anything the dignitaries had ever seen before. The uniform was sleek, fitted, and muffled every move the wearer made so that nothing could be heard when he made his entrance.

"This is the final version of our ultimate weapon," the chancellor said. "This... armor, for lack of a better word, is unlike anything we've ever produced before. To be brief, it amplifies the natural ability of the user. Senses, instincts, agility, strength, speed, and of course sorcery. This is everything we've needed. Not only will this level the playing field, it will give us an extreme advantage. When we face those abominations again we will annihilate them."

"That sounds incredibly impressive, Myamar, but

how do you know it works? Still more important, how can you be sure it will work against the dragonborn?"

"We know it works because we've tested it," the chancellor said, arrogant as ever. "We've been testing it for eighteen years."

"Eighteen years? Well, why haven't we heard of it?"

"You have. We've been steadily and systematically blowing up the city of Taline for almost two decades. All those 'terrorist attacks?' That was this armor, going through round after round of rigorous testing and remodeling to create the perfect weapon. For the perfect war."

"Myamar, have you lost your mind? If Stefan were ever to find out about this—"

"He hasn't discovered anything in eighteen years and I have no reason to believe that will change now. Besides, if he ever does find out I'll implicate each and every one of you as just as culpable as I am. If I go down, I'm taking all of you with me. Perhaps that's incentive enough to keep this conversation between friends."

"So, it's blackmail then?"

"It's self-preservation. And while the method may seem cruel, I assure you you'll feel differently when you're able to walk over the cold, dead corpses of our enemies. We know this armor will work against the dragonborn because we tested it on one who was enrolled here. Andie Rogers. We used her icon to steal bits of her DNA and although we were unsuccessful in turning her genes into a weapon, we did succeed in creating a weapon that disintegrated the specific dragonblood DNA sequence. In short, if you use this suit against a dragonborn, effectively, there won't be anything left of them.

"Now, I've sent out the herald. The seven great families of Arvall will finally be together again soon. It will be the first time in nearly two hundred years that we've all been in the city. Until then, my friends, rest easy knowing I've secured our future."

Myamar held up his arms to the assembly and they applauded him. Maybe from fear, maybe from genuine gratitude. They would have done anything to get rid of the dragonborn. Shortly after that, the meeting was closed and the dignitaries left, still smiling. The man in the armor followed Chancellor Mharú through the room and back to the chancellor's private office, one of many which the University kept for him.

"We're alone now," the chancellor said. "Feel free to take the cowl off."

The man removed the cowl and his long hair fell to his shoulders; he hadn't cut it in quite some time. He'd also recently started growing a beard, though it was only just long enough to stop being shadow. He was tall, lean-muscled, and had grown fiercer in the last months than he had ever been before. He'd become the leader of the chancellor's armored battalion and of the many things he wanted, perhaps the most pressing was his desire to serve Chancellor Myamar Mharú.

"I'm very pleased with your improvements," the chancellor continued. "When you first applied for the battalion, I was rather hoping you'd screw up so that we could kill you. Everyone wanted you dead. At first I marveled at your ability to transcend that and now I've grown to respect it. You've come farther than anyone in these last months and your efforts will not be forgotten."

"Thank you, chancellor," the man said. "Permission to speak freely."

"Of course."

"I wonder, chancellor, if the other dignitaries and heads of state would be so willing to follow you if they knew that this was all part of a much larger game. I mean no disrespect, but I worry what their reactions might be when they find that you've done these things in large part for personal reasons."

"You mean to satisfy my own political aspirations? My dear boy, they already know. Just as I know that they will follow me because they think it's best for their own futures. Those men and women who just left certainly aren't the smartest you'll ever meet, but there are no illusions among them. Everything is a political ploy, every decision a carefully planned stroke, every word and handshake a play for future prestige. Politics is not a career, it's a lifestyle. True, I advocate hate against the dragonborn. However, it's not because they pose a threat or even because I personally hate them. I do it because they're a familiar evil that the people can unite behind and once the people are united I'll be there to step into the role of their savior."

"So, you don't think the dragonborn are dangerous?" the man said, unsure of which questions were appropriate to ask his superior.

"Of course, they are," the chancellor responded. "But every living thing is dangerous in its own way. My family has hated the dragonborn and their beasts for centuries. I certainly don't like them, but that kind of pervasive enmity is from another time. I'm an opportunist. If the dragonborn hadn't decided to come back I would've chosen some other group of people to persecute. I want you to understand something, my friend. Knowledge is important. It's why I worked so hard to turn one of Andie Rogers' friends against her to feed me information from the inside of their little rebellion. But contrary to popular belief, knowledge isn't power. *Power* is power. Never forget: we're not after the dragonborn. We're after control of Noelle."

"I understand, chancellor," the man said with the

conviction and acquiescence of a true soldier. "I pledge myself to your cause."

"And will you die for my personal gain?"

"No, sir. There'll be no need for that. No one who comes between you and your destination will survive me."

"Oh, I like you," the chancellor said, reclining in his chair. "We're going to make a great team you and me. Your name is... what, again?"

"Ashur, sir."

"Ashur. I like it. I apologize, I'll have to make a better effort to remember it."

"Nothing to apologize for, sir. I knew it would take people a while to learn my new name."

"And why did you change it?"

"Because who I was before wasn't good enough. That person was a failure. He's dead now. Ashur lives."

"Excellent. That'll be all for now, Ashur. While you're out today, head over to Taline and test the suit out some more. We wouldn't want Stefan to get bored."

Ashur gave a slight bow and then walked out, closing the door behind him and leaving the chancellor alone to continue his evil schemes.

"I like that name," he said to himself. "I'm glad he changed it. 'Tarven' was a rather stupid name anyway.

I think I like the idea of self-reinvention. I may have to consider it myself."

The chancellor reclined in his chair again, arrogant, grinning, and thinking on all the evil he had planned. For quite some time, he had been planning for this. He'd made a series of very grave mistakes in the early years of his political career and all but tarnished the family name. The fact had never left him, had always been hanging over him like some dark curse. And so, many years ago, the chancellor began planning the events that would eventually culminate in a massive war.

Unlike most people, Chancellor Mharú knew everything about himself and accepted it. He knew he wasn't the most well liked, or the bravest, or the best sorcerer. But what gifts he did have were equally as powerful if wielded correctly. He knew he was patient, heartless, and persuasive. More than anything he knew he was a coward, and, because he could accept that, he grew very close to the concept of fear. He knew what it looked like, how it operated, what potential it could have. He knew he'd never get where he wanted to go on his name or his ability, so he planned to capitalize on the fear of others. He had originally planned for a civil war a few years from then, but when he heard the portal that trapped the dragonborn was becoming active he adapted his plans.

He knew it was all a lie. He knew the dragonborn were a peaceful people. He knew it and his ancestors knew it, too, but they didn't care. The chancellor wanted to grind Noelle into nothing through its own fear, then rebuild it in his own image. He wanted control of the land and the people, from coast to coast. He knew what a dangerous game he was playing, but he also knew that he was the only one who knew all the pieces and all the moves. He wasn't coldhearted because of circumstance or necessity. He was simply evil.

CHAPTER TWELVE

ANDIE AND YARA STILL HADN'T SPOKEN TO EACH other. They couldn't—there was too much hanging in the air between them. Andie was thinking that she didn't even know the girl in front of her, didn't trust her and wasn't sure that the girl hadn't tried to kill her or transport her back to the University. As she watched Yara, Andie figured she must have been just as confused about this meeting. Yara must have doubted Andie's power, her ability to protect herself or more importantly any of the fighters who had signed up to fight with her. Andie knew that Yara had essentially always thought that Andie was invincible. Andie herself had thought that some days. But after seeing her sent from the ship so easily—maybe she had been the one to do the sending—Yara must have doubted Andie's ability.

Yara was the first to move. She took four cautious steps toward the door and then stopped, as if waiting for Andie to make the next move. Andie walked all the way up to the door. And then opened it. She didn't know what she was doing or why; all she knew was that the girl in front of her had once been her closest friend, her most loyal ally, and now she didn't even know if Yara wanted to kill her. Yara's expression seemed to suggest that she was thinking the same thing.

Without thinking it, Andie closed her hand into a fist. The fist started to glow and vibrations swam in the air around it. Andie hadn't meant to do it. At least she didn't think she did. When Yara saw the fist, she took a quick step back and began to emit her own light. And suddenly the tension between them was incredible, impossible. The gulf dividing the two girls had never been so vast, so insurmountable. Andie was hardly aware of what was happening. All she knew was that she felt so betrayed by the person across from her. The girl she'd recently found out had killed. Then, almost as quick as she could blink, Andie shut the door, brought the spell back up, and hurried out of the brig. Raesh and Saeryn were waiting for her at the top of the stairs.

"Good talk?" Raesh asked.

"Honestly, I don't know what that was," Andie

said. "Are you any closer to figuring out who it is? Do you have any leads?"

"Nothing. I think it might be best to hand it over to someone more objective. Someone who doesn't know them as well and isn't related to two of them."

"Which among them is even powerful enough to cast such a spell?" Saeryn asked. "Casting a spell like that, even targeted at a single person, requires a massive amount of energy. I would suggest looking at the older ones first."

"The oldest one is my dad and he's a human. The next oldest is Andie's dad, and we know it wasn't him because he wasn't with us in the caves. Murakami has some magical ability, but her blood is not pure so I don't know how strong she is or could be. Carmen and Yara are both incredibly powerful. Kent has always been kind of ordinary, while Sarinda and Lilja are two of our best fighters. However, I can't say for certain what the three would be capable of if they'd gotten secret training. They're quick learners and fierce combatants. So again, we just come full circle."

"Whatever happened, it was serious magic," Andie said. "When I woke up, my body was weaker. It was like the three weeks I'd jumped had all been spent without sunlight. Like my body was confused."

"What really troubles me is how this imposter knew where to send you," Saeryn mused. She leaned against the wood-planked wall, her arms held casually behind her back. "I don't think I would be wrong in assuming your destination wasn't common knowledge?"

"Not at all," Raesh said. "It took me a week to even get the captain to tell me where we were headed. No one has been allowed in his control room except the first and second mates, and the captain is the only one with a key. And he never leaves the coordinates in plain sight. Not even the first mates should know where the ship is headed."

"Then the spy must have gone directly into Andie's thoughts. It is cruel and reckless magic, but it tells us that this spy is not to be toyed with. It would be very unwise to underestimate this person."

"We won't," Andie said. "Where were you planning to go after here, Raesh?"

"If we were able to find the dragonborn we were going to head back to the source. Arvall City. If we can stop the lies there, then we can stop the vicious rumors in their tracks. Overcoming the University and Arvall should be our top priorities. There's no way the University could go ahead with its designs if it can't get the support of its own city. And from there it's a domino effect."

"You make it sound simple, but it's going to be the hardest thing we've ever done. These people have been having nightmares about the dragonborn for hundreds of years. And the University took that fear and multiplied it. Every day we wait the lies grow stronger, become more real. I don't know what we're going to do."

"You're going to bridge the gap," Saeryn said. "Between your time and ours. You'll have to convince them that we're good, that we mean well, and that we seek the same peace they feel they now have to fight for. We want nothing but to find a new home and begin to rebuild. We are not the monsters and it's important that they understand that they are not the monsters either. Aside from a few obvious differences, we're really not so dissimilar. But I won't presume to teach you how to do your job, you're already sacrificing so much. I won't take your autonomy on top of it all. I have faith in you."

"So, Arvall?" Andie asked.

Saeryn offered a small smile. "To Arvall."

The three nodded and there wasn't much to say after that. Andie walked Saeryn back up onto the upper deck. Oren and the captain had moved outside and were discussing something in great depth. Oren looked thrilled to see Andie, and even happier to see that Raesh was not with her.

"I think our best bet is to go back on foot," the captain said.

"What?" Andie said. "Why? We can't go back on foot that would take too long."

"Oren here was telling me that the river turns south a few kilometers further."

"But I thought it went straight until it hit the coast?"

"I'm afraid that was our doing," Oren said. "In creating our caverns and tunnels we've had to displace a great deal of soil and stone. In addition, the erosion of the lowest peak has pushed the river into a new direction."

"But that shouldn't matter anyway. We can just turn around and go back the way we came."

"We can't, Andie," the captain said. "The Nathair has one of the strongest currents in Noelle. If we opened the ships engines to their max we could probably fight a good way back, but with the ship working that hard we'd run out of fuel before we even made it halfway. Even if we did have the fuel, I'd never try to push the ship through the Gray Fold coming from this direction. It'd be suicide. If we keep on the direction we're going now, at a moderately increased speed that will cut down time but not burn too much fuel, we could make the coast in two weeks, but then we have to sail all the way around the bottom side of Noelle to get back to the port at Arvall."

"Captain, are you telling me that there's not a single stream or river we can take to get back any faster?"

"This isn't a commercial river, Andie. The current

is just too strong. Once you're on it you're on it until your reach the end. There are a lot of tributaries, but they're all flowing too strongly in the wrong direction, making too many delaying twists and turns, or too small."

"How long will it take to sail around Noelle, once we reach the coast?"

"At least three weeks. We've got to travel down the coast and then turn west to come around. We turn north when we pass New Carthage."

"I'm terribly sorry for our inconveniencing you," said Oren.

"No, it wasn't you. Even if the river was still running the way it used to, we'd be in trouble."

"How long would it take you and the passengers to cross on foot?"

"I would take a few days to cross these lands safely. After that it would simply depend on what kind of transportation we could get. I'm not familiar with the area, but this is the most rural part of Noelle and I doubt if anything is coming through this region that can carry all five hundred plus of us at once. So, I'm guessing we'd be walking most of the way."

"That's too long," Andie said. "We need to get back now. We've already waited too long."

But they were out of ideas. They knew that the University was already preparing to reopen soon as a military training ground and that would be the end of everything. The dragons could cover the distance easily and rapidly, but there was no way the creatures could carry the dragonborn warriors and the Council fighters. The dragons were strong enough, but there wasn't enough space. They talked it over a bit more, but when nothing viable came up they decided it was finally time to call it a night.

"Andie, we'll come back and speak with you tomorrow," Saeryn said. "Enjoy your time with your friends."

"Actually, I..."

Andie didn't know how to say what she wanted. She missed her friends, all of them new and old, but there was no possibility of her staying on that ship overnight. She'd told Raesh that she would be staying the night, but she hadn't meant it. When he asked her, he'd had a look on his face that almost begged her to stay with him; he seemed as if he was either afraid himself or was totally against her going back up on the mountain with Oren. Andie wasn't an idiot. She'd noticed the looks they'd been giving each other, which was stupid because she didn't even know Oren, and Raesh was... Well, Raesh was Raesh.

Truth be told, Andie did want to stay with Raesh. Just to talk with him and laugh with him, and maybe pretend for just a night that things were the way they used to be when she was a scared first-year student at the Academy and he was the flirty-but-sweet boy who helped his father around the restaurant. But she couldn't stay on that ship, not with a traitor on-board who was potentially one of her closest friends. She didn't know who to trust. And if the traitor truly had as much power as they were beginning to believe that person did, then Andie couldn't risk getting others get hurt in an attempt on her life.

"I'm going to go back up with you," Andie said, raising her voice as several bolts of lightning came down nearby. "I don't know who to trust on this ship and every time I think about it, it just gets worse."

"But what about your... what about Raesh?" Saeryn asked.

"He'll understand," Andie said. "Will you tell him, captain?"

"Of course."

Andie mounted up behind Oren, and he and Saeryn lifted off and cut through the flashing sky. As the lightning curled through the air around her and the thunder ripped through time and space, Andie began to seriously think about the future of the fight. For all she knew the traitor could have converted others by now, could have devised an entire plan to wipe them all out before they made the coast.

The spy had the advantage of anonymity and of knowing exactly what the University was planning. The only kink that had happened so far was that the person had been locked up because they got too eager and performed the spell in the same room with Andie. But if the person managed to find out Andie's destination without being in the control room, there was no definitive way of saying that they had to be in the room in order to cast the spell. She simply didn't know what to think.

When they finally made it back to the mountain, Andie went straight to the area that had been given to her to live in. She said some parting words to Saeryn and nodded to Oren, and then left in such a way that everyone knew she was asking not to be bothered again that night.

Andie tried to think of a plan, any plan with any outcome, just something to keep her mind busy, but she couldn't. All she could think of was the peace of mind she'd lost and all the lives on that ship that were suddenly susceptible at the hands of a traitor. She wondered how someone could be that evil.

It was easy to understand why Chancellor Mharú and his cohorts were so against the dragonborn: they had been raised to hate them. They had known nothing but that hate since birth and since the dragonborn weren't around to defend themselves, the people had no reason to change the way they felt. But the traitor had lived among people who felt otherwise, people who knew how kind and how beautiful the dragonborn were. This person had made a conscious decision to brutally betray everything and everyone surrounding them. They had put the lives of hundreds of Council fighters at stake and could potentially doom the dragonborn if not unmasked soon. And if the traitor was successful and provided the University with the things it needed to grow, that would be the end of Noelle as they knew it.

And the University itself was a whole different kind of evil. They were proud of the systematic genocide that had been carried out centuries before and wanted to bring it back again. They had no proof that the dragonborn were who they thought they were —they just wanted them dead, gone. Andie couldn't believe she had ever trusted that place to teach her, to educate her about her own people, her own power. Failing to get anything done, physically or mentally, Andie put out her light and laid down.

But sleep did not come. Her mind wouldn't stop working, worrying. And when she finally did manage to forget about those things for a moment, a crushing nostalgia set in. What she wanted more than anything that night was to make things revert to the way they used to be. She wanted to go back to Michaelson, before the Academy, before dragons, before the battle in the Archives, before that little room over Marvo's restaurant, before her father's accident, to the time when she and her parents were a family. When they were whole.

She wanted her mother back, the woman she was

forgetting more and more as time went on. Sometimes, late at night when she was alone and pretending to be asleep, Andie could almost feel her mother's arms around her. She could hear her voice, smell her, and even see her there next to her, smiling. But most of the time that woman was a kind of void inside of Andie, something that had existed too long ago to leave as lasting an impression as she wanted. Andie wondered what her mother would have to say if she were there with her, if she could see the way the world was so eager to hate and slow to accept.

Andie knew the University wanted to win the unanimous support of Noelle before opening the military facilities. Raesh had told her about some of the news they picked up along the Nathair. The University had almost finished constructing the newest facilities and adapting the old ones. Soon it would become the perfect training place for killers driven by fear. It would also become the perfect fearmongering institute, undoubtedly the first of many.

The University knew how to manipulate fears— they had been doing it for five hundred years. She could almost see Chancellor Mharú sitting at his desk, smug and satisfied, thinking that the battle was practically won. The only thing that scared her where that coward was concerned was his resources. The chancellor may have been cravenly, but some of his associates and interests were not. He had access to hundreds of years of magical knowledge, relationships, money, tools, infrastructure, and more. All Andie had was her power and her allies, and the latter was in an unreliable state.

Thinking of the University made her think of Tarven, the other coward and traitor, though the only person he had betrayed was Andie. She would never admit it out loud, but she thought of him every night. She liked to think of him and some days she even looked forward to it—not because she felt in any way romantically linked to him, though. She thought of him in order to keep herself fresh, sharp, at her most aware. She never wanted to be caught in the open like that again, which was part of the reason why her current situation was hitting her so hard. Thinking of Tarven forced Andie to face her mistakes, her bad judgements, all the forgiveness she had heaped on him until the last possible moment when it was almost too late and almost cost her the lives of her friends. Tarven had played her like an instrument, had toyed with her and blinded her. She never wanted to feel that again or be the kind of person who forgave the unforgiveable, or ignored her own instincts just for the sake of preserving an illusion she knew in her heart wasn't real. As she thought back she realized just how far she had come in a short period of time. It hadn't even been a year since the fight in the Archives.

CHAPTER THIRTEEN

"I want to tell you a story."

Andie nearly jumped out of her skin. It was Saeryn. The Queen had crept up without a sound and was standing behind Andie, smiling and waiting patiently for the girl to respond.

"Saeryn, I didn't hear you coming."

"I'm a dragonborn warrior. You never know I'm there until it's too late," she said, taking a seat.

"Let me make a space for you—"

"No need. I may be a Queen, but I'm not spoiled. A little dirt is good for humility. Now, I want to tell you a story and I don't want you to interrupt. You can take whatever point you want from this story or you can forget it entirely. It will be your choice. I only want to share it with you because I genuinely believe it will be of some help. Also, you're a terrific listener,

Andie, and your heart is full of hope, no matter how bitter you may want to seem on the outside. Do you accept my terms?"

"I do," Andie said, leaning back on her arms and waiting for Saeryn to begin.

"Well, good. This is a story about me. I wasn't always a Queen. In my time, I was just a girl. Truth be told, I was little more than a peasant. Much like you, my mother had been killed by fanatics from the University and I lived with my father. In those days, the dragonborn wouldn't think of hiding, even though we had already been scared into submission. Some cruel mind had invented the Sentinels, the only things I've ever seen that can kill a dragon. Our poor, beautiful creatures began to fall all over the regions.

"My father and I were farmers. We grew crops, raised animals, and did some modest pottery. We never had much, but we always had each other. It was rather nice, actually. But, of course, the University wouldn't be sated by any amount of carnage, no matter how terrible. Eventually they came to our region and enslaved or butchered everyone. The last time I saw my father I was being ripped from his arms. You see, though we were considered lesser, savages, the sorcerers sometimes kept the women and girls around for their pleasure. I didn't hear of my father again until some years later, but of course they'd killed him the same day they took me.

"I was fortunate enough to fall in among a group of older women who had been slaves for a while already. They took to me and protected me. For three years, they looked out for me and kept me from the filthy hands of the sorcerers. Those were dark times, Andie, and we suffered terribly. There was no relief for me even in avoiding the lechery of the sorcerers. Torture, starvation, humiliation. There aren't words for some of the things we endured. And the sorcerers just kept hurting us, figuring out new and innovative ways to bring us pain because our dragonblood kept healing us. But as you know, though we heal we still feel pain. We still feel every second of pain. I can't tell you how much it broke my heart to see those women going in my place, offering themselves for those nightmarish evenings instead of letting the perverted sorcerers have me. They would cover me in mud or rub me down with molded food to make me less appealing. They were my angels.

"I'd only passed seventeen winters, but I had no intention of being a slave all my life. I knew I need to escape and knew that somebody needed to unite my people, give them hope. I already knew that I came from a long line of royalty, but by the time I was born our people had been thrown into disarray. Even my mother never got a chance to sit on the throne. By the time I was enslaved, our people weren't concerned with royal lineage, only survival. In fact, there were many royal lines. I'm proud to say that mine was the kindest. Even dragonborn had cruelty in their history, but my royal line had always been fair and understanding.

"One day the guards came for me. I had made up my mind to go with them that night. I refused the mud, the rotten food, and all the other tricks the women had used to keep me safe. Three years was more than enough time in slavery. The women cried as I was dragged off, but I knew what I was doing. The sorcerer who kept us was so wealthy I don't think even he knew how much money he had. His palace was so large, it took twenty minutes to reach him from the slave gallery. When the guards dumped me at his door he looked me over, then made me bathe. I let him watch me, let his eyes drink me in. I relished the bath. I had not been fully clean since I'd left home. I washed my body, my hair, cleaned my teeth and feet. When I was ready I went to stand by the bed; I beckoned him, pretended I had accepted my fate. He did not know what I planned.

"I won't tell you how, but I will tell you that I disposed of him in a manner I thought fitting. I snuck back to the slave gallery, told the others what I had done, and offered them a choice. We found our strength and from then on, we fought back with everything we had. It wasn't long before we had completely overrun the palace. We left there and divided into groups, liberating our people in multiple regions. I grew in influence and my power grew as well, as I ceased to be afraid.

"Before I knew it, I was a general in our militia. We began to understand that the only reason the sorcerers had defeated us physically was because they had first defeated us mentally. We had let them frighten us. We had cowered in their shadow. But that was done. Soon we were uniting in the mountains we had previously called home and not long after I was given the great honor of being asked to reign among our people. I didn't want the throne at first; it seemed silly to stand on ceremony and call myself a Queen when we were fighting for our lives and didn't even have a permanent home. But I did as the people asked. If it had not been for Eitilt, that terrible curse, we would have taken back our world, yet that was not the turn fate had planned for us.

"I know you have many questions and concerns, not the least of which is why you were the one to hear our call for help. That answer is... complex. As are the many 'whys' behind your betrayer's actions. Such is life. You fret too much. I will go now, but I leave you with this: we are a powerful people, Andie, and there is no limit to our power when we choose to abandon fear and leap into hope."

Saeryn smiled and touched Andie's hand. They sat

like that for a moment, not speaking, not moving, just understanding. When Saeryn finally stood to leave and Andie was left alone, she felt significantly better. At the beginning of her stay, Andie had felt special in having Saeryn spend so much time with her; she felt that she had been singled out by the Queen. However, the longer she stayed the more she began to understand that Saeryn treated them all that way; she genuinely loved her people. Then Andie had begun to wonder how she could have such grace under pressure when there were thousands of things that could go wrong and millions of people wanting their ultimate destruction. But now she was beginning to understand. Saeryn wasn't optimistic or willfully blind. In fact, she was acutely aware of the many ways in which their way of life could be ended, but she understood that her strength wasn't for herself. It was for all the people watching her, the people who depended on her in order to believe that what they were fighting for was worth it. And that's when Andie finally understood.

Pain was probable. Fear was merely possible.

THE NEXT MORNING, Andie was feeling better; she couldn't fool herself into ignoring her circumstance, but she realized that there was so much more than just her personal feelings involved. She also knew that no matter what was going on onboard the ship, she had her people, the dragonborn, behind her.

She straightened her space and then went out to see what her people were up to. That morning the children were performing a piece they had been working on in their classes. Andie was amazed that the dragonborn had set up a school, markets, and a prototype of a financial quarter in less than a year. They had already mapped the entire mountain range and were fast approaching the initial phase of their building projects. They were going to take a group of the smaller peaks and break them down into materials they could use to construct buildings, aqueducts, and a number of other things as well, all of which would unite to create a formidable infrastructure. They had also already begun mining in the mountains and the valleys between. They had found a number of useful minerals, silver, coal, and even iron ore. One of the architects told Andie all of this and more as they sat and watched the children perform.

When the performance was over, Andie went to the market to get food for breakfast. The dragonborn didn't deal in money, at least not among themselves: everyone had a set of tasks and as long as everyone did their share the workload was light and resources were plentiful. She was amazed at their ability to share, at the evidence of their evolution beyond petty scheming to a kind of generosity and compassion that

Andie could hardly describe. It was like being in the middle of one big family. One enormous, incredibly content family. Of course, they had arguments and disputes—in fact, Andie had witnessed at least four such instances since she had been living with them—but they resolved them with reason and love.

Michaelson had been her home her entire life. It had always been a paradise to her, with its gold and waving fields, the lake that stretched toward her like an old friend, the sky endless and open above her. And, for a time, she had called Arvall City home, with its glass and steel and opportunities, its history and its diverse people. She'd found a second home and a great system with Marvo and his family. But being up there on the mountain with her people felt more than right. It felt like destiny.

"Andie, one day you're going to have to leave this little place. It's not right for you to stay here, cloistered and afraid of the world."

"I'm not afraid, dad, I just don't see what the big deal is. You're a sorcerer. Why can't you just teach me how to control my magic? You lived with mom, she must've told you some stuff about how this is supposed to work."

"There's no way I could ever replace your mother or do the things she would've been able to do. She could've taught you everything you needed to know, and with ease at that. My magic is totally different

from yours, Andie. Even at sixteen, you're already as strong as I am. This time next year you'll be more powerful than me and in ten years you'll have more power and ability than I could ever dream of. I love you and I wish I could keep you here with me forever, but you need to learn control."

"Fine. Then I just won't use my magic at all. I don't want to leave you here alone. And I don't like the city. It's loud and it smells and the people are rude and you can't see the stars at night and—"

"And you don't want to go. And I don't want you to go. But, Andie it's about more than just learning control. You need to learn about your history: who your people are, what happened to them, what your future could be like, what you're capable of. There's only so much I can tell you and even your mother didn't know much about the history of the dragonborn. You have to know that I would do anything for you, but I can't make the world accept you or what you can do. You need to learn how to hide your magic. And don't argue because you know I can't handle the thought of something happening to you."

"I don't have to go now or soon, right? I can stay with you a little longer?"

"Of course you can. It's still a couple of years before the Academy will take you, but one day, sweetheart, you'll have to go. It won't be so bad. You can visit me and I'll visit you. but Michaelson is such

a small part of the world. And you're meant to do great things. One day you'll find it."

"Find what?"

"Your destiny."

Thinking of her father almost brought Andie to tears, but she was also incredibly happy to have him back with her again. She was planning to talk to Raesh when she saw him again and make sure he understood that her father was coming with her, back up to the mountain. He wouldn't spend another night in a cell, not even to appease the other fighters. They must've known that he wasn't a spy. As she walked, she looked around her at all the life and happiness and she knew that her father would be happy there. The dragonborn might not let him stay long, but as long as the ship was in the vicinity and as long as her people would have him she wanted him to see what she'd found. She took her armful of items and set them down in a crook of the mountain where the sun was shining perfectly.

She began to put together a modest breakfast and bathe in the soft light of the high sun. Not long after she began, a dragon landed not far from her and curled its huge self into a ball to sleep. Its steady, deep breathing was almost hypnotic and it helped Andie relax as she finished preparing and began to eat.

She was content. She looked around her, watching the stillness and the grandeur of the mountains. She looked behind her and saw a thin, climbing pillar of smoke, no doubt from one of the new caverns been blown out with dragon fire. For a happy people, the dragonborn were surprisingly hardworking. They understood the totality of requirements in order for them to preserve and protect their way of life—they accepted it and went on with the business of living. Andie finished her breakfast and got up to go find Saeryn.

They saw each other at almost the same instant. There were smiles, waves, and Saeryn turned her body and her attention to the approaching Andie. She was almost to the Queen when a mighty roar rang through the sky. As one, the dragonborn turned to the sky and so did Andie, all of them watching the dragon as it soared with a greater speed and a fiercer determination than Andie had ever seen. Everybody on the plateau cleared out of the way as the dragon landed so forcefully it cracked the ground. The warrior who was riding dismounted and looked as if he had seen something terrible. He turned left and right, searching, until finally his eyes landed on Saeryn and Andie.

"What has happened?" Saeryn said, her shoulders already clenching to bear the weight of the new burden.

"There has been an explosion," the warrior said. "We were out beyond the range, watching over the

Nathair to see if anything had entered to region. We heard a noise, a terrible noise. It wasn't until we turned and flew back along the river that we realized it was the sound of steel being torn apart. The ship..."

And with that he looked at Andie and she immediately felt the knots forming and twisting in her stomach.

"The ship carrying your friends," the warrior said. "It's been ripped in half."

CHAPTER FOURTEEN

"Explosion?" Andie said, barely focusing. "What happened? Is anyone hurt?"

"I'm afraid so. There were casualties. I'm not sure to what extent, but I don't have a good feeling about the outcome. I came back to alert you. The two who were on patrol with me have stayed behind to watch over the wreck from a distance. We couldn't go down, in case whoever or whatever did that was still there and still posing a threat."

"What do you mean *who*?"

"I'm dragonborn. I know fire and explosions. Whatever happened there wasn't an accident. No natural explosion could have done that. That was magic. Dangerous magic."

"We must go down at once," Saeryn said, taking Andie's arm. "Gather all the healers and tell them what has happened. Have them meet us at the ship immediately. Bring food and water. Gather blankets, clothes, and be as quick as possible. Where is the ship? Did it move at all from its position yesterday?"

"No, it's still there. What's left of it."

"At once."

Saeryn began to run with Andie still in her grasp. Andie could barely comprehend what was happening. All she could think about were the names. Raesh. Yara. Eric. Marvo. Carmen. Kent. Lilja. Sarinda. Captain Wolfe. Charles. Murakami. Sarah. Elizabeth. Mary Louise. Roderick. So many people who had aligned themselves to her cause and gave up their lives to be there on that ship, fighting for what they believed was right. Over five hundred brave souls who had given up a life of ease to fight what had never been a fair fight, and now they may have given up their lives entirely.

Before Andie could understand what had happened, she was on the back of a dragon riding behind Saeryn and they were plunging through the sky. Andie had meant to ride behind Oren, but had mistaken Saeryn's dragon for his; for a split-second, Andie thought she saw a strange look on Saeryn's face. But, of course, there was a strange look. There was a strange look on everyone's faces. They had just found out the people coming to help them were probably dead. Saeryn gripped the dragon differently, more purposefully, and the creature seemed to sense her desire. Andie had never experienced such speed and power before. The dragon was a living breathing knife in the sky and in seconds they had passed through the ominous clouds and left the sunlight behind.

Beneath the clouds, the lightning seemed brighter, hotter, faster than ever. The thunder sounded a thousand times amplified, so loud it was like each clap traveled down inside of her and split her again and again. The dragon flew like it was honing in on something, unaffected by the lightning, heedless of the thunder. Andie had finally come around and brought herself back into her body, back into the midst of yet another horrible incident. This was all the University's fault. They had planted the spy and told them to wreak this havoc on the unsuspecting fighters. Andie just couldn't comprehend how anyone could be so evil, so hungry for other people's blood—at least, she hadn't understood it until right then and there as she was cutting her way through the sky.

Suddenly she was filled with a rage and a bloodlust unlike anything she'd ever known was possible. She hoped that of all the lives lost, the traitor would still be alive. She wanted to see them, touch them, feel their throat beneath her hands. She had never relished the thought of violence, and certainly not of taking a life, but she had reached her point and passed it. Whoever the traitor was, they had performed their last evil. She prayed for them to be alive. She prayed for the chance to end them.

As they neared the ship's position, Andie was finally able to see what the warrior had warned them about. The other two dragons were still circling above the wreck, but when they saw Saeryn and her group approaching they came down to join them.

The ship itself was a complete ruin. It was split open about a third of the way along its length. The wreck was lying on the edge of the shore where they had anchored before. The explosion had blown the steel back in sharp, grotesque tears. The shining grey steel of the ship abruptly became a smoldering black at the split, the long, jagged shards of steel point out from the point of the blast. Only a thin sliver of the bottom of the ship held the two halves together, but even so there was nothing that could be done for it. Andie was in a kind of sedated awe when she saw it, the great bulk of the ship lying on its side in the sand, the lightning running the sky above.

But as they came closer and closer, Andie began to see that there were survivors. Lots of survivors. They were standing or lying along the shore, wounded, anxious, looking up at the dragonborn in fear as if they thought they were being attacked. Saeryn turned the dragon to fly over the wreck to survey it from the air. Totally destroyed. The survivors were tending to each other and Andie searched desperately for a face she recognized. She searched for her father. Finally, the dragon touched down and Andie leapt off.

She ran through the people, looking at their injuries, their lacerations, their wounds, their blood. They reached out for her, tried to question her or garner some reassurance from her, but she couldn't stop. She simply couldn't ask her legs to quit moving until she had found a familiar face. Finally, someone seemed to understand what she wanted and pointed. She followed the direction of the finger, and, even when she didn't see anything, she just kept running. Hoping. And then there he was.

She couldn't tell who reached who first. All she knew was that she was in Raesh's arms. Or maybe he was in hers. There was one less person she had to worry about.

"Where are you hurt?" she asked, checking him over furiously. She spun him around in front of her, examining every inch of his body as he turned.

"Andie… Andie, I'm fine. I caught some shrapnel in the side, but I'm fine," he said, stopping his spinning and placing his hands firmly on her shoulders. "I've already been seen to. Andie, it wasn't an accident. It wasn't natural."

"I know, they told me," Andie tried to hide the frantic emotion from her voice. "What happened?"

"One minute everything was quiet. Then suddenly

there was a horrible flash of heat and the floor began to rise. A moment later, the ship was ripped apart." Raesh's eyes were haunted, the memory clearly burned in his mind.

"How many dead?" Andie asked, already afraid and tensing to receive the blow.

"Eighty-seven."

Eighty-seven people dead, because of her. She hung her head, but Raesh pulled her in again. He held her, tried to comfort her. She could hear him in her ear trying to reassure her, trying to convince her that this wasn't all her fault, that he didn't blame her, that no one blamed her. But that didn't matter to her. She wanted blood. She pushed away from him.

"Who did this?"

"Come with me," he said.

He took her hand and led her through the crowd. The fighters still tried to get her attention, to get *her*. Andie was beginning to wonder if they wanted her help or her blood. Raesh led her to a clearing that she hadn't noticed from the sky, where a group of people lay together, side by side. But Andie's eyes went behind them, to her father. He was alive. She ran to him and threw her arms around his neck. Her heart was finally able to slow as she held him, knowing he was real and was okay. She leaned back to look at him, and, aside from a fairly serious wound above his eye, he seemed to be fine.

163

"Andie, I know you're going to want to make a fuss over me, but I'm fine. I swear to you. Raesh moved me last night before any of this happened. He knew I didn't belong down there. And you have more pressing issues to attend to. All these people are looking to you right now and you need to give them something. Deal with this. I'll be here. Go."

Andie wanted to protest, but she could see in her father's eyes that he was serious. She nodded, kissed his cheek, and rose. She turned to look at the bodies on the ground. Carmen. Kent. Murakami. Sarinda. Her heart froze in her chest. She knelt down, prepared to mourn, but realized that they were still alive— breathing raggedly, but still alive. She could have died right then and there from the relief.

These few seemed so much worse off than the other survivors. As Andie pushed Carmen's hair back from her face, she saw that the face was covered in blood, a series of slashes cut across her beautiful face. Her breaths came slow and ragged, and she remained unconscious as Andie stoked her hair. It crushed her to see Carmen like that, but she felt a wave of relief to know that Carmen wasn't the traitor. That also meant that Kent, Murakami, and Sarinda were innocent. Andie looked around for Marvo, anxious to exonerate him as well, but she couldn't find him. There was a moment of fear as she realized that if he wasn't hurt there was a good chance he might be... She looked to Raesh.

"Where's your father?" she asked. "Please tell me... don't let... is... is it him? Is your father the traitor? Did he betray us?" She hardly recognized her own voice as she asked the questions, willing beyond anything for the answer to prove her wrong.

Raesh looked at her in a way he never had before. She knew it was true when she saw his eyes. Raesh was broken, defeated, only holding himself together because he had the weight of the rebellion on his shoulders. Andie wanted to reach out for him, but she couldn't. She was broken, too.

"I can't believe this," she said. "I can't believe this."

"Andie," Raesh said, his expression indefinite, his lips fumbling, his hands shaking. He paused. "My father is dead."

Andie lost her breath. A kind of stasis took over her.

"We couldn't tell what happened at first," Raesh continued. "We thought he might have... escaped... but... we found what was left of him. He's gone."

Andie tried to will herself over to Raesh. She sent all kinds of commands to her body to get it to move, or think, or communicate, or do anything at all. But she remained suspended above herself, numb, and instead it was Saeryn who went to place a comforting hand on Raesh's quivering shoulder. He stood there, his shaking hand placed over Saeryn's, barely even strong enough to hold himself together. He then fell to his knees and buried his head in his hands as Andie and the rest stood there, watching their friend mourn his father.

And then Andie broke, again, but this time it was rage that bubbled up from the wound. She looked around and around and around until she found her. The traitor. The only one left. Lilja.

Andie walked over to her and Lilja saw her coming. Lilja stood up and curled her fists, ready for whatever Andie would do. Andie cast right at Lilja's face, but it was blocked and countered and a ball of red light collided with Andie's chest. That made her even angrier. As she and Lilja began their duel, the other fighters all backed away and cleared the area, ducking the stray spells that went streaking through the air. Lilja was more practiced than Andie had thought and provided a challenge. Lilja seemed to understand how furious Andie was and she refused to go without a fight.

Andie quickly grew tired of the annoyance. She raised her hand and slammed it into the earth, and it was hard to tell which was louder, the thunder or the sound of the earth breaking out from Andie's hand. Lilja was blasted up and off her feet, and, when she came back down, she landed directly on her spine against a stone. She cried out in pain, but before she could even roll over, Andie was already standing over her. Andie raised her hand, and, with her magic, took Lilja by the throat and lifted her into the air. She began to close her fist, which began to close Lilja's throat from every direction.

"Andie, stop!" her father called. "Andie, you can't do this!"

"Leave her be," Saeryn spoke kindly but raised her hand to Andie's father. "Too much has been lost this day. Justice is only right, though if you can, Andie, try not to kill her. She must pay, but there is a way she must do it. A duel is one thing, murder is another. You are not a murderer."

"Murder?" said Andie. "You're going to tell me that I shouldn't kill her? Look around you. Eighty-seven of our own are dead because of her. My friends are lying there near-dead. And Marvo... Marvo... She needs to die! This is the University doing everything it can to break us, to make us afraid, to crush us before we can even get on our feet. For weeks, we've been living in fear, afraid to trust each other, unsure of whether or not we would even make it. She cursed me into the future! She created chaos and split us all up! She needs to die and I'm going to kill her!"

"I'm sorry."

Andie turned her attention back to Lilja. The girl's

face was beginning to change colors and she was kicking at the air, trying to free herself.

"Let me explain. Please," Lilja said in barely above a whisper.

"Andie," Saeryn said, her hand on Andie's shoulder. "Let her speak. She may have information we need."

Andie wasn't interested in hearing what Lilja had to say, but Saeryn put her hand over Andie's and brought down the arm and the magic. Lilja came back to earth and as Saeryn put Andie's hand down, Lilja was able to breathe again and began to take her air in gulps. Andie stood tense and furious, ready to exact her vengeance at the first chance.

"I didn't do this," Lilja said. "I swear it wasn't me."

"Liar!" Andie screamed and used her magic to push Lilja over.

"Andie, enough," Saeryn said in a new voice. "Calm yourself. Look at the girl. Can't you see she's terrified?"

"I didn't do this!" Lilja shouted. "I'm sorry for the thing I did, I know it was wrong, but I had no choice. Please, you have to believe me."

Andie watched the begging girl. She was thin, blonde-haired, pale, and beautiful in a classical kind of way. Ever since Andie had known her, Lilja had been frowning or scowling, completely loyal to the cause, yet still arrogant and conceited. But as she looked down on her there by the river, Andie realized what she was seeing. Lilja was afraid. No, not even afraid. She was petrified.

"Tell us the thing you did," Saeryn said. "And fear not. I will see that you are punished for no more than you deserve. If mercy is merited, it will be given. You have my word."

Lilja looked up at Saeryn with tearful eyes and swallowed hard as she rubbed her throat with both hands. She finally nodded. "I only helped them the one time," she pleaded. "Just the once. When we were hiding in the tunnels. I went up to scavenge with Sarinda and a group of Searchers caught us. They called the professors and one of them recognized me. They threatened my family. My friends. I might have signed up to fight this fight and to risk my life, but my family didn't. I couldn't just let them be slaughtered."

Andie took a step back as she looked down at the girl. She was trembling all over, her eyes glazed over with the horrors of what she had done. Andie took in a deep breath and let it out slowly then knelt on the ground next to Lilja. "Go on."

"The Searchers said they would let them live if I told them where we were and how they could find us," her voice was hoarse, barely a whisper. "I told them we were hiding in the tunnels under the University, but I never thought any of us would die. I thought that because we had you and Raesh and all the fighters that we could take them and make it out safely. I figured they didn't even have a chance against us. I swear, when we came out, I fought them with everything that I had. But that was it. That was the one and only thing I ever did for them, I swear. I've been trying to atone for it ever since. I've been doing my best to make this mission work."

By then, Lilja was in tears and Andie was relenting. She could see that no one could have been harder on Lilja than she was being on herself.

"So, it was you and Sarinda who told them?" Andie asked.

"No, Sarinda never said a word. She didn't have any family so they couldn't make her cooperate. They wiped her mind. She doesn't even know she was with me. Andie, I know you and I have never gotten along, but I only did what I thought I had to do to keep the people I love alive. And when we were on the ship I did my best to stop the other one."

"The other what?"

Lilja held her head in her trembling hands as she held back a sob. When Andie placed her hand on her shoulder, she took in a silent gasp. Finally, her trembling stopped and she steadied her voice as she looked Andie in the eye. "The other spy."

Andie was dumbfounded, as was everybody else.

"There's another spy for the University here?"

Andie asked. "How? Who?"

"I don't know. When they had me they just told me that they already had someone else working in our group and that it was only a matter of time before we imploded. They laughed about it. They said they chose this person because of you. That once you'd been brought down, you'd be easy to wipe out. I swear I thought I could figure out who it was and stop them. I never thought they'd be powerful enough to send you to the future or blow up the ship. I'm so sorry. I'm so, so sorry."

Andie turned from Lilja. She raised her eyes and scanned the crowd. That left one other who could possibly be the traitor. One other who happened to be in that room when Andie was blasted away. She didn't want to believe it, but she had no choice. She scanned the river side with keen eyes until she saw her lying still some distance away. Andie began walking over and a path cleared in front of her, fighters moving aside as they watched her expression. She made a straight line over to the girl and when she reached her, Andie just looked down on her.

Yara was covered in blood. And even though she surely knew that Andie was standing beside her, she wouldn't look up. Andie spread her fingers and pushed toward Yara. The blood that covered her began to disintegrate, turning into dust and then drifting up into the lightning-filled sky. Soon Yara's face was clean, as was the rest of her. Andie searched briefly with her eyes, but could see nothing.

"I don't even see a scratch," she managed to whisper. "You're not hurt at all, are you?"

Yara turned her face up toward Andie, slowly, methodically. She spoke in a measured whisper.

"No."

Andie dropped to her knees. She vaguely heard people talking behind her, someone giving commands, yelling, moving feet. She went numb, deaf, mute, immobile. Her eyes were frozen on Yara's face, as Yara's were frozen on hers. Eighty-seven dead. Hundreds injured. Lilja a traitor. Carmen gravely injured. Marvo dead. The ship in ruins. And Yara. Yara. Andie just kept watching her, unable to do anything else. Her skin felt like ice as she stared into the eyes of the girl who was once her best friend. Once a trusted ally. A traitor.

Then out of the corner of the sky a green dragon came diving right toward them. It was Ronen. Yara was totally oblivious of it. The dragon leveled out several yards away and flew straight for them, its great mouth open. Suddenly it had Yara between its teeth and it was flying away with her, straight up into the dark sky, weaving its way between the unremittent lightning.

Andie was aware only of her body falling over. Then darkness.

CHAPTER FIFTEEN

"Everything will be ready in three days, Chancellor Mharú. The Sentinels, the army, the propaganda. All of it."

"Excellent, Ashur. I am completely in awe of your transformation. You've taken a fledgling program and made a master work of it. Your dedication will not be forgotten. When I come into my kingdom, I will remember you."

"Your praise is reward enough, chancellor. The only other satisfaction I need is to see the dragonborn eradicated. This entire plan is yours, from start to finish, has been executed masterfully. I'm just happy I was allowed to be a part of it. I'll go and bring them in now."

Ashur turned to go, and the chancellor prepared himself to receive his guests. The seven families had not been together in a very long time. Chancellor Mharú was the last of his line and had been under tremendous pressure to marry and continue his family. And he certainly planned to, but before that could happen, he needed to touch it. True power.

The other families had quietly ruled their respective domains for many years and never once had any issues; this fact had teased them into thinking they were competent and while they were certainly more effective than the chancellor, the truth was that none of the families had faced the challenges that Myamar had. They had never given a formal reason for their leaving, but he knew it was because of the portal. They knew their ancestors had barely managed to capture the dragonborn before and even then, it had cost the world greatly. They were afraid of the thing, afraid it would open up again and the dragonborn would wreak terrible havoc on their lives.

But the chancellor had never wanted to live anywhere else. His family had moved generations previous, but as soon as he was a man he moved back to Arvall. He had made it his responsibility to manage the city from which they all came. For many years, his staying was the only positive mark in his long list of embarrassing mistakes. But all of that was about to change. Just as he had settled into a pose he thought was welcoming, but also formidable, Ashur reappeared.

"Where are the families?" the chancellor asked.

"They're refusing to see you, sir."

"What?"

"They say you haven't yet proven yourself worthy of their presence."

"How dare they! Do they have any idea what I've been through? What I've done to get here?"

"I'm sorry, chancellor. I insisted, but they said it was impossible. They won't see you until you've done what you promised to do and eradicated the dragonborn. They say they don't believe you have the power or... forgive me, chancellor... the courage to carry through on your claims. They only came to see the University out of nostalgia. They're going to be staying up in the professors' quarters in the mountain. They've asked that neither you nor any of your administration bother them until the task is done."

Chancellor Mharú was so furious he began to get hot. He swiped his hand across his desk and knocked everything off onto the floor. He threw his hands up and magic cracked the ceiling and blew the windows out. He collapsed into his chair and buried his face in his hands. He wanted to issue orders to Ashur to bring the families forcibly down, but he was too full of rage to speak.

Ashur waited respectfully. He wanted to ask if there was anything he could do to serve the chancellor, anything he could do to make the situation more manageable, but he had seen the chancellor like this before and knew it was best to wait.

Suddenly a sound began to come up from the chancellor. It was a moment before Ashur realized what it was. The chancellor was laughing. He was actually laughing. The chancellor began to laugh so hard that for a moment Ashur wondered if the man was beginning to lose his mind, but then Chancellor Mharú looked up.

"Kill them," he said. "Kill them all."

"Right away, chancellor," said Ashur unhesitating and pleased. "How would you like it done?"

"Use the new armor. Hopefully, the irony won't be lost on them. And Ashur?"

"Yes, chancellor?"

"Make sure they suffer."

Ashur bowed, turned, and left the room. The chancellor twirled in his chair to face the window. With a casual wave of his hand he fixed the glass in the window, though he left the crack in the ceiling. Somehow it brought him joy. He spent a few moments fantasizing about the cruel, slow deaths of the other families. He was certain that from that day forward there would be nothing and no one to stand in his way. The old days were done and Myamar Mharú would never again be thought of as a coward.

Just that morning he had worked one of the most powerful spells he had ever performed. It was truly a masterpiece and only he and Ashur knew of its occurrence. The only thing that bothered the chancellor now was thinking about how the spell had affected its target. He had a specific goal in mind, but one never knew how these things would turn out. He thought about his spies living among the rebel fighters and he trusted that they understood their place in the plan. Of course, he was planning to kill them along with everyone else. There was no room for loose ends in the empire he was planning.

The chancellor stood and left his office. He greeted the aides sitting at their desk on his way out and walked down the long, shimmering hallway that lead toward the front of the University. The new banners and schedules had already been hung up for the fast approaching opening of the military training grounds. The chancellor smiled at the banners as he strode arrogantly past. The damage from the night of the battle of the archives and from the escape of the rebels had been cleaned up. The chancellor had his administration working around the clock to put away even the memory of the University's failure. He had even issued a gag order covering both the events.

THE SAME NIGHT of the battle in the archives, the chancellor had sprung into action. He may have lacked basic courage, but he was nothing if not resourceful. He knew with so many people fleeing the building and the dragonborn wreaking havoc in Leabharlann, it was the perfect opportunity to exact revenge. Most of the dignitaries in the mirror room had opposed some of his more extreme measures. They had called him everything from a demagogue to a fascist imposter. He grabbed Ashur, who still called himself Tarven then, and headed for the mirror room. As he suspected, the dignitaries had remained in place, doing their best to exude elegance and calm while the commoner folk were hurrying out. There was confusion and chaos all around, as nobody was yet sure of what was happening. All they knew was that there had been explosions and a group of professors had come running and screaming out of the library. One of the foreign heads of state approached Myamar as he entered the room.

"What is the meaning of this? The festival is being ruined by this tumult. Explain yourself."

The chancellor ignored him and moved on to inspect the room. He turned to Tarven.

"How fast will your plants work?"

"Almost instantaneous," Tarven said, still trembling in fear. "What do you want me to do?"

"I'm going to clear this room of everyone who hasn't pissed me off and then I want you to kill the rest. Give me a moment."

The chancellor hurried to the small dais set up at the side of the room. He grabbed the microphone.

"All students and guests need to leave the room immediately. Proceed down the hall and out into the front lot. There's nothing to worry about, just a small gas leak and we want to get it checked before things escalate. All foreign heads of state and dignitaries need to remain here for a moment, as we have special evacuation protocols for you."

The chancellor waited patiently until everyone unessential had cleared the room. Just as the last of them were leaving, the other dignitaries from outside were being brought in by the professors. The chancellor had asked that they be rounded up. When he finally had them all in one place, the chancellor looked out to survey the crowd. He was performing a last check to see if any of them were worth saving. He saw several of his friends among them and even a few of his distant relations, but he was not a man to be swayed by that. He smiled.

"If you'll all just wait here for a moment, we'll have someone come in who will show you a quicker, less bottlenecked path. Wait here for your much-deserved treatment."

With that, Chancellor Mharú stepped down from the dais and headed for the door. He nodded to Tarven, who was still struggling to pull himself together. Tarven turned and waved his hand at a section of the flowers he'd placed earlier. The petals began to blacken and disintegrate, and as they turned into Ashur a white smoke began to flow from them. The chancellor, Tarven, and the remaining professors exited the room. The dignitaries, who were no fools, saw the smoke and immediately tried to follow the chancellor out, but they found themselves blocked by an invisible wall. The chancellor turned to smile at them as his spell trapped them inside the room.

"I'd like to give you a dramatic, fitting goodbye," he said. "But you're not even worth it."

He turned to leave and the people in the room looked up at the flowers; all the way around the top of the room the flowers were turning black, becoming Ashur, and pouring the white smoke over them. There wasn't much time after that. Soon they were all dead. The chancellor's only regret was that he hadn't had all of the dignitaries in the room at the time. Apparently nearly 300 had already left the building before they could be rounded up.

As the chancellor rounded the corner, the screams began to reach him. Ashur and his battalion must've caught the other families before they boarded the train to leave. The chancellor relished the sound of death and magic. He was more confident than ever that the new armor would prove more than a match for the dragonborn if it could defeat the families. All seven of the family lines were extremely old and extremely powerful, not to be taken lightly if one valued your life. If the armor could best them in an honest battle, it just might defeat the dragonborn.

"Chancellor! Chancellor!" screamed one of his assistants as they came running through the hall. "Something is going on at the train. The battalion... they're killing the families!"

"Killing them?" Chancellor Mharú asked. "As in defeating them? Murdering them?"

"Yes! There's blood everywhere and the families are trying to escape, but the battalion won't let them. It's a slaughter!"

"I understand your sentiments, it's very distressing," the chancellor said, trying desperately to hide his smile. "But the battalion is only performing its duties. Evidence has recently come to light proving that the families are actually traitors in league with the dragonborn. I asked them here to give them a final chance to come over to the right side and they attacked us. The battalion has no choice but to eliminate the threat to the University. It's to protect us, all of us. Even you."

The girl still seemed anxious, panicked, clearly not used to seeing much blood or violence. She was shaking uncontrollably and by now had begun to cry. Chancellor Mharú took her gently by the arms and looked into her face.

"Go back to my office. Have one of my aides make you some coffee and try to settle down. Don't think about what you saw or heard at the train, okay? Put all of that behind you."

"I can't forget that. I can't stop... hearing those voices..."

"Listen," he said through gritted teeth, grabbing the girl hard and giving her a violent shake. "If you want to work here you need to get used to seeing these kinds of things. People will die here. A lot of people. There will be torture, pain, suffering, dark magic. There will be blood. If you can't handle that then maybe it's time for you to do a little suffering of your own. Now get out of my sight."

He tossed the girl aside and kept walking, not even looking back to see if she was alright. The cruelty made him feel powerful.

Once he was outside, the chancellor walked straight across from the University to the very edge of the precipice and looked down on the city. The whole vast grid was under his influence, his lies, his propaganda. All he need to do was make the people afraid and after that they belonged to him. They would support anything he wanted, as long as he could kill the dragonborn and their beasts. And if he actually did manage to kill the dragonborn, then all of Noelle would be his.

Just then he heard a scream and the sound of running feet behind him. He turned. It was Rasputraenir, current head of the House of Urania. He had managed to escape the battalion and was running, running, running, straight for the chancellor.

"Myamar! Myamar, you have to help me!" the man cried. "They're going crazy in there! They're killing us, they're—"

But before he could finish, the chancellor waved a hand and the man was lifted into the air, flipped, and thrown over the side of the mountain. The chancellor didn't even bother watching the body fall. Instead, he simply enjoyed the sound of the man's final scream.

"Everything is mine," he said, his eyes on the city.

CHAPTER SIXTEEN

WHEN ANDIE WOKE, SHE DIDN'T KNOW WHERE SHE was, at first. Her mind was clouded, her head hurt, and she felt nauseous. But within seconds everything that had happened came rushing back in. She bolted upright and found she was lying in her living space, on the mountain. Someone had spread her bed out for her and there were two little cups beside where her head had been. She threw the cover off and jumped to her feet. As she turned, she came face to face with Lymir. It startled her.

"Lymir," she said. "What are you doing here? How did I get back on the mountain?"

"Well, it's a hard tale," he said, taking a seat. "The way I heard it was ye fainted down there by the river. I don't blame ye, not after what happened. They gathered ye up an' flew ye back up here for a good rest. I haven't left your side since. I give ye some tea to make ye sleep an' I've been wi' ye ever since."

"Where is she?" Andie asked. "What have they done with Yara?"

Lymir looked down at his feet and for a moment he refused to meet Andie's eyes. She moved closer to him and lifted his face.

"Lymir, tell me what happened."

"They've sentenced her to death, Andie. I'm afraid..."

Andie felt like she should have said something, anything. But she knew there was no point. She turned from Lymir and began to straighten up her area. He watched her and tried to talk to her, but she responded to nothing. Then he tried to help her clean up, but she refused and asked to be left alone. Hesitatingly, he left.

About a half hour later, Andie emerged from her space and went straight for Saeryn.

"How soon can we be ready to leave for Arvall?" Andie asked.

"Are you sure that's the best thing for now?" Saeryn asked. "I agree that we need to leave as soon as possible and make great haste, but you have quite a situation at hand. Hundreds of your friends are injured, some dead, and of course there's the issue of the traitor."

"I understand it's not ideal, but you know as well

as I do that we need to stop the University. That's what all of this has been for. All the suffering, and enduring, and betrayal, and lives lost, everything was leading us up to this moment."

"But Andie your people—"

"Knew what they signed up for. I'm not happy to see them like this: broken, injured, betrayed. But they knew the risks. They understood that they might not make it home again or if they did they might not be the same people who left. We are at war, Saeryn. This is the cost. And while I am beyond grateful for everything that they have given and sacrificed, they are not my people. You are. The dragonborn are."

Saeryn did not look convinced, but she gestured for Oren to come.

"Oren, have the warriors prepare. We leave within the hour."

Oren nodded and disappeared around the bend of the cavern. Saeryn remained and watched Andie, looking her over from head to toe. Andie felt herself being watched, but she wouldn't meet Saeryn's eyes. She could feel everything Saeryn wanted to say, every emotion she was feeling. Pity, compassion, sympathy, fear, anxiety, love. Saeryn had told Andie that when two dragonborn were especially close, they could sometimes sense each other's emotions. Andie hadn't realized until just that moment how much she and Saeryn meant to each other.

"Andie, I already know what you'll say, but you should be here for it."

"For what?"

"The execution."

Andie gave a small gasp. The word made her feel cold. Numb.

"She made her bed and now she needs to... They can do it without me. I don't need to be a part of it."

"You know, there were traitors in our time as well," Saeryn said. "And many of them were friends and people I trusted. It was hard to have to watch them die, but somehow I knew it was my duty to be there. Betrayal never ends, not really. They turn their backs on you, betray you to your enemies, and then force you to have to kill them. That's the worst part of all because then you feel guilty for punishing them, even though you know you had no choice. And you continue to feel guilty for the rest of your life."

"Saeryn, I can't. I just can't. You and the rest of the dragonborn call me your savior. You lift me up on a pedestal and act like I'm some kind of miracle. You say I'm the one who can bridge the gap between our people and the rest of Noelle. Let me focus on that. Give me the chance to be everything you and the rest of our people already think I am. Let me earn your trust. But, please, please, don't ask me to stay here and watch her die."

"As you wish," Saeryn said, touching Andie's

arm. "I'll call for you when we're ready. You will ride with me."

Andie bowed and turned to leave. She went outside to be alone and found herself in the very corner of the mountain where she had been when the ship exploded. But she didn't think about that. She didn't think about Carmen and Murakami and the others lying unconscious in the sand. She didn't think about her father's terrible wound. She didn't think about Marvo's death or Raesh's pain. She didn't think about the ship, the victims, the blood, the unbelievably agony and blackness of that entire circumstance. She didn't think of Lilja. And she didn't think of the traitor.

Not much later, Saeryn found her. She took a seat beside Andie and they simply sat there in the sun, in silence and uncertainty.

"Raesh can handle things down at the ship," Andie said.

"And your father?" Saeryn asked. "I think his wound may have been more serious than he let on. With him already being in such frail condition, I fear for him."

"I just want to get out of here," Andie said, standing.

Saeryn gave up after that, though she seemed hurt. She led Andie to where the dragon warriors were gathering with their dragons. Lymir tried to get

Andie's attention, but she ignored him and mounted up behind Saeryn. When all the warriors had mounted their dragons, they all left the ground behind. Oren was to stay behind and oversee the execution, but would join them after the deed was done.

A faction of warriors and healers had also been left behind to watch over those who were staying on the mountain. The scientists, thinkers, teachers, farmers, and other important contributors were to remain behind, as well as the children. They weren't terribly concerned about being defeated in battle, but Saeryn was a wise and careful ruler, and she did not want the future of her people to be left to chance. She wanted to be prepared for any outcome and to ensure that the dragonborn would never again be in danger of extinction from the earth.

They flew like they had never flown before. They soared so high in the sky they couldn't be seen from the ground. Andie held on tight and every time she thought the dragons couldn't go faster, they surprised her. They truly were incredible beasts. Before the sun set they had left the Hot Salts of Mithraldia behind and were making great haste over vast rural regions that Andie didn't recognize. The sun sank behind the horizon and still they flew on, as efficient at night as they were in the day. Andie allowed herself to be filled with the energy of flight. It kept her mind from going to places she didn't want to think of.

The dragons were flying as fast and deliberate as ever, not the least bit tired, but the dragonborn treated their dragons like they treated their family and so they soon came down to earth and landed in a field that had recently been harvested. The bent stalks were a perfect place to lay for the night. The warriors all dismounted and saw to their dragons, then everyone went to sleep almost at once. They would need to rest and be back up in the sky before the sun came up. They couldn't risk being seen and spreading fear before they reached Arvall. They had no plan, not even a definite beginning of one, and the last thing they needed was for their surprise appearance to be ruined. Neither Andie nor Saeryn slept at all.

In the morning, just as the sun was beginning to lighten the sky, the dragonborn took up again and rose to their usual height. On and on they flew, passing mountains and valleys and woods that sometimes seemed to go on forever. They passed a lake so blue and deep and dark that it looked like the night sky had taken liquid form and fallen to earth. They flew over small villages that could barely be seen from the sky and they came to cities whose building were so tall they had to circumvent the city just to be safe. Shortly after midday, they settled in another field to rest and were soon off again. They mounted up again and followed a narrow but seemingly endless river. They flew as if a demon chased them, cutting the sky with blinding and confident grace. Never once did they break their formation, they were so disciplined and focused. Andie was certain that whatever they met in Arvall would be no match for them.

Night came again and they settled to earth once more to rest. The dragons were able to drink from the river and some of the warriors washed their faces before eating and lying down. Saeryn laid down and was asleep instantly. Andie watched her, knowing she must have been exhausted from the stress alone. She knew that as much as Saeryn valued her help and support, she wanted more for Andie than just fighting for a cause. But that would have to wait. There was too much going on at the moment, but the most pressing issue was the University and its inability to let the past go, to stop spreading lies and leave the dragonborn to live in peace. Andie felt her own body warning her it was becoming dangerously low on energy, but as long as she kept getting enough sunlight in the daytime she would be fine. Besides, she couldn't possibly think of sleep at a time like this, when the soul of the whole world was hanging by a thread. The University couldn't win. The chancellor couldn't win.

When they woke up in the dark of the morning, Saeryn said that they would arrive in Arvall just before sunset. By flying in a straight line and taking advantage of the dragons' incredible speed, they would do in three days what would have taken the ship more than six weeks to do. Andie didn't respond when Saeryn said it, she just went to the dragon and loaded up again. For the first time in days, she was excited. She was ready to fight the University, to meet them in the street or in the hallway and hand them over to destruction. They had killed so many people and caused so much pain, not only in the past weeks, but in all the centuries that they had been in power. Andie was full of mixed emotions and she relished the opportunity to vent them. She had no intentions of holding back or showing mercy.

The dragons mounted up from their final rest and they took to the sky. They would not touch the ground again until they reached Arvall City. They did not know what they would find there, but they went to face their destiny bravely. Andie looked down on the lands they passed over, knowing they were probably filled with people who hated them, who wanted to see their blood running in the street. It had never occurred to her before that it might not matter to the world if the University had been spreading lies. For all she knew, the rest of the world hated the dragonborn as much as the University and would want them dead anyway. It was no secret that the dragonborn were incredibly powerful; people tended to fear things more powerful than themselves, regardless of whether or not those things or people posed an actual threat. And though the dragons were sweet, calm creatures by nature, their great size and intimidating appearance would put people off. What if the world didn't care that the dragonborn hadn't done anything? What if they were just looking for an excuse, any excuse to slaughter the dragonborn? And if a fight did break out, the dragonborn would have no choice but to defend themselves and then the world would see the true magnitude of their awesome power. If that happened, if the dragonborn were forced to take even one life, the world would never forgive them. Everything would be at an end. They would go to war and the dragonborn would kill thousands, millions, of the sorcerers and common folk in an attempt to save their way of life—and in the eyes of Noelle the dragonborn truly would be monsters.

More than that, there was always the chance that the people would be willing to relent, but simply wouldn't believe Andie. The loose, ill-conceived skeleton of a plot they did have revolved around Andie's ability to persuade people that neither she nor the dragonborn posed a threat. She had to erase centuries of hate, propaganda, and engrained teaching. Even Andie didn't believe it could work. Hatred of the dragonborn was one of those things that simply was. She had no idea what she was going to say.

The land slid away underneath them. Rivers and lakes disappeared somewhere behind them. Things too small and far away to be distinguished flashed by, instantly forgotten. The sun fell lower and lower into the sky until it finally touched the land in the distance. Across the horizon, the great towers of Arvall City were coming into view, shining silver and blue against the land. The sky began to darken as they flew closer. The energy and the mood among the warriors seemed to change as they began to get close to the city. Everyone was bracing for the inevitable, whatever it might be. They slowed gradually the nearer they came and began to drop lower over the city. As they slowed, the sound of the wind and the dragons' wings lessened considerably. Saeryn turned to speak over her shoulder.

"The outcome doesn't matter," she said.

"How can you say that?"

"Because I only just realized it. No matter what happens, Andie, we are forever grateful for you being with us. Thank you."

Saeryn turned back around and then the dragon plunged. The phalanx of warriors followed closely and they were all diving through the air, descending on the city. For a moment, Andie was perfectly calm: the wind raced past her, the massive wings of the iridescent creature pumped up and down on either side of her, the city rushed up with its lights and actions, Saeryn's long dark hair danced in the sky. And just for a moment, before they knew the result and before the conflict started, Andie felt the future was theirs, one way or another.

But suddenly there was an explosion in the air and one of the warriors was knocked off of his dragon. The dragon quickly maneuvered itself back under him and he caught hold, but the first explosion was quickly followed by several more. The explosions were erratic and incredibly powerful. Because the dragons couldn't see the explosions coming, they couldn't maneuver around them and the situation quickly became dangerous. What was most terrifying was that the explosions were black and as cold as a freezing winter. It was smart. Any regular explosion wouldn't have been able to distract a dragon or the warrior on it. Heat made them stronger. But a cold explosion could seriously harm them and with the sun going down it would be harder for them to heal.

The dragonborn began evasive maneuvers, but they were all for nothing as the University's trick continued to plague them through the sky. Andie noticed that there were less explosions the lower they went and pointed it out to Saeryn. Again, the dragonborn dove through the sky. The dragons flattened their wings against their bodies and the warriors flattened themselves on the dragons' backs. They fell through the sky, hoping to reach safety. They finally broke the level of the city's highest buildings and the explosions gave out. The dragons leveled out and headed for Brie. For the University.

The explosions must have doubled as a warning system because as they came closer to the ground, Andie could see people in the streets below panicking and running inside. Cars were racing away, barely missing each other as they sped for safety. And then a horn began to blare. What should have been a quiet landing was turning into a fearmongering nightmare. Saeryn and the dragonborn warriors remained calm and pointed the dragons for the mountain. Andie grew less certain by the minute. Soon they had reached the foot of Brie and were beginning to incline as they began their ascent. The moment was almost upon them now and Andie couldn't think of anything. Nothing at all. She was simply in expectation.

But the University had planned ahead again. Slots opened in the mountainside and sorcerers behind shields of energy began casting spells. As the ill-aimed spells flashed by, Andie could feel the chill coming off of them. They really were beginning to learn. But the dragons easily dodged the feeble attempts and the warriors only cast defensive spells to protect their ascension. Andie was filling with energy. Her mind and heart were still blank, but she was suddenly aware of her own power. She'd stopped trying to understand why and how the University could be so evil, but if they wanted to go to war with her, with her people, she was prepared to do so.

They cleared the precipice and found that the large lot in front of the University was completely full of people. The civilians screamed and ducked as the dragons came soaring up over them. The warriors did a single lap and then landed wherever they could: on top of the University, away on the side of the mountain, and some stayed flying above. Andie and Saeryn dismounted and walked to meet the crowd.

"Saeryn?" Andie whispered.

"Yes?"

"I think I'm afraid."

"So am I."

CHAPTER SEVENTEEN

As THEY APPROACHED, THE OTHER DRAGONBORN warriors began to fall in behind them and the more they walked, the larger their group grew. The crowd that had already gathered began to back up, to clear out of the warriors' way. Andie and Saeryn each kept a wary eye on the people, unsure of what they might do now that they were face-to-face with the threat they had heard so much about. The response was exactly what Andie had suspected: absolute fear. Andie looked around, trying to gather information about why all the people were gathered, but it wasn't hard to discover. There were massive banners strung up all around, posters, and signs with the event. They were there to celebrate the reopening of the University.

Andie looked over and noticed for the first time that all the damage that the University had sustained was fixed and the black marble looked stronger and more sinister than ever. She hadn't realized before, but even SKY 6 had been replaced with a new model and the rails had been repaired and burnished. There was a gated area not far from where they were, and she could see a massive collection of fireworks waiting to be released for the ceremony. There were heads of state standing on a platform in the direction they were heading. And so was Chancellor Myamar Mharú. He didn't seem at all surprised to see them and only then did Andie realize that they had played directly into his hands. He had planned all of this from the start, knowing that blowing up the ship would force them to escalate their timetable and come to face him. Andie felt like a complete idiot.

"I told you they would come," the chancellor began. "I told you they couldn't resist the opportunity to show themselves, to menace us, to do everything in their power to end our way of life."

"I believe you have that backwards, Melpomene," said Saeryn, in that authoritative yet gentle voice that only she could manage. "It is my people who have been hunted and slaughtered, and I am ashamed to see that nothing has changed in the centuries that have passed."

The crowd began to grow enraged, afraid, at the very sound of her voice.

"We did not come here for war, though we are

prepared for it if that is what you prefer. We have only come to expose your propaganda for what it truly is: a snake pit of lies. We have been in this world for months and yet you cannot name a single crime that we have committed."

"A *single* crime?" the chancellor mocked, feigning disbelief. "The list of your horrific accomplishments has no end. You broke the laws that govern our world and breached time through an illegal portal. You slaughtered the innocent people working in this University who only tried to reason with you. You murdered hundreds of dignitaries and heads of state in the mirror hall—the great leaders in this land. You came back again some weeks ago and wreaked even more havoc and how are we supposed to know what chaos you've been creating around the world?"

"If we were truly so bloodthirsty would we have landed our dragons and come to walk among you?"

"It's your own arrogance that put your feet on the ground."

"More lies, I'm afraid. We escaped that portal because your ancestors trapped us in there and our entire race was almost exterminated from the face of the planet. Once we were out, we were immediately under attack and though we wish there had been another way, we had no choice but to defend ourselves. Since then we've been living in the mountains, far from here. If we're so horrible why have you heard nothing of us for months? And we never returned to this mountain until right now. The people who were here were rebels fighting to bring peace and you slaughtered most of them while they ran for their lives. I believe that is what you meant to say."

The crowd continued to bubble and get angry. Andie kept her eyes on them and the warriors were always ready for anything.

"My name is Saeryn. I am the Queen of the dragonborn. I assure you, my people do not want war. As you can see, we haven't even brought all our ranks. This is only a small party that has come here seeking a resolution."

But the crowd seemed to have hardly heard her. They did not see a Queen, only the embodiment of every nightmare and cautionary tale they had been told since they were children. And those who hadn't heard the stories were afraid because everyone else was. Someone in the crowd threw a stone, but Andie blocked it with her magic. More stones followed, but the warriors kept them all at bay until the crowd died down again.

"They will not hear me," Saeryn said, turning to Andie. "I pass the torch to you, savior. If you cannot placate them, it will mean war."

Saeryn took several steps back and let Andie come forward. The chancellor laughed.

"What kind of Queen lets others fight her battles? Are you afraid?"

"I find it hard to believe that you of all people are going to stand there and accuse someone else of cowardice," Andie said. "All of Noelle knows that you lack the courage of a child."

"Remind me again who you are," he said, grimacing. "You seem... inexperienced for a rebellion."

"My name is Andie Rogers and I was once a student at this University. My father was a sorcerer, but my mother was dragonborn and she passed that magic to me. I am a part of both worlds and I can assure you all the true enemy here is not the dragonborn, but the University. When I was a girl, they came to my house and they beat us. They took my mother and nearly killed my father. I never saw her again. Some years later, they arranged for my father to have an accident and nearly killed him again, though that time he never fully recovered. Does any of this sound familiar? Have any of you ever had someone taken from you, threatened, killed? I know they try to wipe our minds when they're finished, but at least some of you must remember."

There were many uncertain mumblings coming from the crowd. They hardly seemed convinced, but at least they were listening.

"These are the misguided and troubled thoughts of

a child," the chancellor said, not losing a step. "If we've ever come to your homes it's only been in service of you. You saw the devastation of the University. Many of you were there that night when we lost so many lives. And it was all because of them."

"Really?" Andie sneered, nearing the platform. "Tell me, if the dragonborn had only just escaped the portal, how were they able have that room filled with poisonous flowers a week before?"

There were gasps in the crowd. They seemed to genuinely want to hear the chancellor's response, but he did no more than smile.

"What's happening now is the same thing that happened hundreds of years ago," Andie continued. "You're letting yourselves be driven by hate and other people's greed for power. Ask yourselves: what have you ever seen the dragonborn do? What evil have you witnessed? Nothing. Everything you think about them was told to you. I know we've all grown up hearing the stories and fearing the legends, but that's all they are is stories. I have lived among you and now I live among them, and though the cultures are different, neither is evil. We could have had our dragons rain fire from the sky, but we didn't. Our magic is stronger than yours and we could have come and started casting instead of talking, but we didn't. That kind of violence is not what we want. All we want is to carve out a piece of the world for ourselves and live in peace. We don't want anything from anyone, especially not a fight."

"That's a very moving speech, little girl, but I hardly think that stories could persist for hundreds of years if there weren't truth to them. Now, people you've seen what kind of carnage results from a world with dragonborn. Read your history books. Look at the painted walls of our corridors. These dragonborn are an ancient evil and they've returned to finish us. Don't be fooled by this simple child's inability to know right from wrong."

"I noticed that in all your aggrandizing, you've never once given definitive proof that my people have done something they shouldn't, or that they've done anything at all."

The chancellor tried to hide his frustration, but his political mask was cracking. He hadn't planned to be caught out like this, exposed. Andie looked at him and could tell that his plan was beginning to falter. He was losing his footing.

"No one has known where the dragonborn have been for months," Andie continued, growing more confident. "We could've attacked you, burned your lives down while you slept and gotten away with it, but we came here looking for a better future. We don't want to have to hide. If you don't want us living among you, we understand, but please allow us to live. There's so much we could teach you, so much we could learn from you. My people have come from a time when everything was different. The new world is foreign to them and they're afraid. We've done nothing, nothing at all."

Much to Andie's surprise, it seemed the crowd was actually listening to her. She paused, afraid to go on and ruin the goodwill she'd garnered, but also afraid to stop before she had them fully. She decided that the best thing to do was tell them not about what the dragonborn *hadn't* done, but about what the University *had* done.

"It might interest you to know that Chancellor Mharú turned two of our friends into spies. He consistently had them place us in danger. Just a few days ago, one of them blew up the ship we had been traveling on. Eighty-seven of my friends were killed and all because this man's greed was insatiable. If you don't stop him, there's no telling what he might do."

Andie leveled a finger at Chancellor Mharú. Before anyone knew what was happening, the crowd had turned to the chancellor and was waiting to see what he would say in his defense. But all he did was stand there, his eyes locked wide in surprise and rage, his legs beginning to shake in front of all the people. Andie almost smiled—the faces of the crowd began to change and the murmurs began to build. She could tell they weren't yet fully convinced, but the longer the chancellor stood there dumbfounded, the worse his chances grew. Andie looked to Saeryn and the two shared a hopeful look. Then the chancellor began to laugh. Andie nearly toppled at the sound, confused as to how he could find anything funny about this situation.

"You know, I really couldn't turn him," the chancellor said with a smile. "I had to resort to more... arcane methods."

"Him?" Andie asked, confused.

"Yes. Your traitor. Oh, wait... do you mean to tell me you still haven't figured out who betrayed you?"

"It was Lilja and... a girl I used to believe was my friend."

"No, no, no, no, no. I always knew you'd catch Lilja sooner or later. She never wanted to cooperate, you know. But once we threatened her family and her friends, well, she started to see things from our side."

More gasps went through the crowd. The chancellor paid them no attention and though Andie was glad the tide was turning, she was hardly able to focus on anything outside of the chancellor's words.

"But the other one wasn't a girl. It was a man. The one with that godawful name. Something so short and stupid I always forget. Marvo. That's it. You see, I knew he would be perfect. Old, human, ridiculously likeable, and an intensely close friend of yours. Not to mention the leader of your little rebellion. The absolute perfect candidate. See, I captured Marvo long before you ever even saw that stupid portal. We were watching you from the beginning, Andie, and when we got wind of what you were searching for in Leabharlann I started making a plan in case you ever managed to free those abominations. Me and a few of my associates kidnapped your Marvo and performed some very old magic on him. It allowed me to periodically act through his body, influence his decision-making, even make him perform spells on occasion. Things like having him decide to stop looking for a way out and bring you all into an ambush. Or having him read your mind whenever you touched him. Or sending my magic through him to send you back here to the University, though, admittedly, that particular spell backfired. Or, my personal favorite, exploding him with a wave of collective magic too large for his body to handle and killing scores of your friends in the process."

Andie couldn't even respond. All she could do was stand there and stare at him, her whole life over the past week being unfurled and rewritten. Marvo. Yara. She'd had it all wrong. And poor Marvo had been used as nothing more than a pawn and then disposed of in the most brutal way possible. All to get to her.

"So, you see, the girl is right," the chancellor said, turning to the crowd. "I am the villain of the story. I did lie and deceive and murder. These ignorant dragonborn may be powerful, but they're essentially harmless, probably not all that different from yourselves. And I did lure them here with a rather intricate plan in order to have my battalion murder them. And I think I'll murder you, too. After all, you're only a few hundred common folk from the city. No one will miss you. You're going to be slaughtered just like those eight hundred people I killed in the mirror hall."

The crowd began to panic and turned to escape, but the chancellor's battalion had slowly been enclosing the entire area while Myamar and Andie had been talking. Now Andie looked around and saw that they were surrounded. She'd expected there to be some kind of opposition waiting, but this was far more than she'd thought possible. The slow-moving, sleek armored men were closing in from all around. The dragonborn warriors tightened their ranks and moved to protect the Queen, but Saeryn waved them away. She wasn't afraid to fight.

"Whatever happens, do not attack," she said. "Only defend."

As if in response to her words, the chancellor clapped his hands and the battalion began their attack. As the first spell hit her defensive shield, Andie could tell that something was wrong. The spell had nearly taken her off of her feet. She knew there was no way a sorcerer's magic could be so strong, so fierce. She looked around and she could tell by Saeryn's face that she noticed it, too. All around her the dragonborn were struggling to maintain their defenses. Their shields were giving out faster and their footing was less stable; the closer the men in black came, the tighter the dragonborn had to retreat. Andie and Saeryn were also using some of their power to shield the crowd from any stray spells.

"Something is wrong," Saeryn said. "They cannot be this strong naturally. It is impossible."

"It must be the armor," Andie said, ducking. "Another one of the chancellor's little ideas. We have to figure out a way to stop them or else defending won't be enough and this is going to turn into a full-fledged battle. What about the dragons?"

"Perhaps. If it comes down to that. But I want to avoid that as long as possible. Seeing the dragons breathe fire will only frighten the people and the dragon fire is so strong I fear it may injure the innocent."

Andie began watching their attackers, searching them for weak spots, mistakes, anything that could give them the upper hand. Then she noticed how all the men were facing them directly, their shoulders squared to the dragonborn. They were absolutely refusing to show their sides or backs. Andie curved a spell between two of the attackers and hit one in the side. There was no affect and it only seemed to make the man that much angrier. She aimed another spell and this time purposefully missed by a wide margin, but she caught the spell once it was past the men and brought it down again so that it caught him square in the back. The man lurched forward and collapsed. However, it was only a moment before he regained his feet and resumed the attack. But the secret had been seen.

"That armor is incredibly strong, but it's vulnerable from the back," Andie said.

Saeryn nodded and cast a spell that bounced off of the ground and curved, catching a soldier in the back. As he was thrown forward, Saeryn cast again and threw him backwards.

"Curve your spells," she called out. "But don't hurt them. Remember who we are."

CHAPTER EIGHTEEN

THE DRAGONBORN TOOK THE QUEEN'S COMMAND AND began a fiercer defense. The chancellor didn't like that. He began to see just how wrong he had been about those people. Still, the dragonborn had their work cut out for them. Saeryn's command not to hurt the battalion members greatly restricted what the types of spells the dragonborn could do and the battalion was incredibly strong. Andie was struggling to fend the men off, as their attacks just seemed to get harder and harder to defend against. But just when things were beginning to look down and Andie was about to suggest they begin their own attacks, a wonderful thing happened.

The people joined the fight. They began attacking the battalion, fighting alongside the dragonborn. At first, Andie didn't know what they were doing and she nearly attacked one of the people as they stepped forward, but then she saw how they took up ranks beside the dragonborn and began to defend against the attackers. The battalion was certainly a force to be reckoned with, and the increase in the number of magical attacks against them didn't seem to daunt them, but it did make a difference. At the very least, it stopped their advance. Not all of the people joined the dragonborn. Some of them remained unconvinced of the lies they had believed their entire lives and took up with the battalion.

Soon, everyone on the mountain was fighting. The air was thick with flying spells that lit the night with their color and energy. Explosions, whistling, and breaks rang through the night as the spells hit home or missed. Only the chancellor remained on the outside of the fight, hiding behind the platform like the coward he would always be.

Andie and Saeryn were fighting back to back and drawing a strength from their proximity to each other. Andie soon realized that they were actually synced and feeding one another through a magical connection that could only be felt between two dragonborn. The fight raged on and on, and some of the civilians from the city proved to be surprisingly powerful casters. But the University's armor was a formidable thing and the battalion soon figured out what the dragonborn were doing. They closed ranks, tightened, and realigned so that it was nearly impossible to get them in the back. and then they unleashed an attack more vicious and determined than anything Andie had ever encountered. They advanced with a maniacal method, refusing to back down or be swayed by the faces of the people they were attempting to kill.

Andie knew that something needed to be done. The air was growing thick and cloudy with the flying spells, the dust, the stones and earth being blasted high into the air. And the dragons were getting restless. They sensed their riders were in danger and they began to crawl about and circle the confrontation while their mouths began to smoke as the opened their great and terrifying jaws. The situation was quickly spinning into something so dangerous it bound to end in a massive loss of life. Andie began to push herself, to think of something that could stop this before it took a turn for the worst.

"Battalion!" one of the men called. He had a red star on his chest. "Attack formation Delta! Offensive maneuver Zero Hour!"

"What is this?" Saeryn asked.

"I don't know, but let's stay close together. I don't like where this is going."

The man who had called out the order stepped forward and took off his mask. Andie had been shocked more times than she could count over the last week, but as she saw Tarven's face for the first time since the night of the battle in the Archives, she couldn't help but to be shocked again. And, this time, all the way down to her core. From what she could remember, Tarven had been in deep with the University and had failed them one too many times. She always assumed that he was executed shortly after the battle and she never thought she would see him again. She never wanted to. Yet there he was, looking stronger and more menacing than ever. He'd clearly left his plants behind to take up the University's new armor, as well as the mantle of leader of their battalion. He looked right at Andie.

"It's been a long time," he said.

"Not nearly long enough," Andie replied. "Honestly, I'd kind of hoped you'd died."

"I almost did, but I've been reborn. Remade into something stronger, faster, more powerful. I'm a thousand times better."

"Well, that's very cute, Tarven, but I'm in the middle of something right now. I'll deal with you later."

"Tarven is gone. My name is Ashur, taken from the transformation of the flowers that killed a room full of useless diplomats and impotent demagogues. And, as it happens, I think you'll deal with me now. Form!"

The battalion took its stance in a single, totally uniform movement.

"Mount!"

The battalion interlocked, arms around shoulders to create an unbroken chain. They also grabbed something on each other's backs and turned. Blue veins began to run through their armor and the temperature within the massive circle of soldiers began to plummet. Simultaneously, black tendrils of smoke stretched forth toward the dragonborn and Andie began to feel herself grow week. It was like she hadn't seen the sun in days, weeks, months. The tendrils of smoke were leeching the energy of the sun directly from their bodies.

"Begin!" Ashur shouted.

All at once an almost blinding blue light rose up from the battalion as the soldiers began to chant. The cold and the tendrils were still draining the dragonborn and it was a moment before anyone could distance themselves from their own pain to pay attention to what was happening. Saeryn was the first to realize. She spoke in a whisper.

"Eitilt."

"The time curse," Andie finished, as they both looked up to the sky.

The wave of blue light from all sides met in the sky above them and merged, creating a dome that covered all of the dragonborn. Terror was quickly passing through the dragonborn and even the fiercest of the warriors looked panicked. Andie was afraid, too, but she was almost too concerned with trying to find a way out to notice her own fear. Almost. Just when she thought the situation couldn't get any worse, they heard a great rumbling sound. They looked up again and a tear was opening above them. It wasn't like the portal Andie had saved the dragonborn from. In fact, now that she saw it with her own eyes, she remembered that she'd seen it briefly, for less than a second, when she had been sent to the future. But as she looked up into the tear she could see something. A great, rolling cloud of death coming across the land. It was the same cloud that had almost killed the dragonborn before Andie pulled them out. They weren't sending them to the future, they were sending them back to the moment before the cloud hit. They would be killed instantly.

And then the panic really began to spread, not merely among the dragonborn who had experienced this before and knew exactly what would happen if they got taken up, but also among the civilians who were trapped in the dome and had no idea whatsoever what was going on. Even Saeryn, who had always been calm and elegant under pressure, was struggling to maintain her peace. Andie wanted so badly to resolve it the way Saeryn wanted, to show the people through sheer force of will that the dragonborn did not pose a threat, but the time for peace was over.

"Saeryn, we can't do this," Andie said, on her

knees from cold and the smoke. "Your way won't work. They're too strong and too ruthless. If we don't fight back, we're never going home again."

Saeryn turned to Andie and looked in her eyes.

"Saeryn, please. You were right. Our duty is to our people and right now that duty is to make it back home to them. We tried to reason with them, but it's over. At least now the people have seen what the University truly is. Now we don't need to convince them. We need to save them."

Saeryn looked around at her warriors, her people. She also gazed around at the civilians who had come over to stand with them. They would all be dead in minutes. She turned back to Andie.

"Then let us do it your way."

She turned back to face their attackers and took a deep breath. As she exhaled, she pushed a massive blast of hot, magenta magic out. The chain of soldiers stumbled and one of them slipped. The tear above them shrunk a little.

"Attack the battalion!" Saeryn commanded.

With that the dragonborn rose to their feet again and began to mount an attack. The soldiers were strong and they were well trained, but the dragonborn were from a time when everything was decided by battle and blood. As they moved out to cast at closer range the battalion began to retreat, the chain began to break as they were forced to defend themselves.

Andie and her people fought through the cold, the smoke, the pull of the space-time tear in the sky above them. They did not cast at any civilians, but their mercy toward the battalion was at an end. Soon the soldiers had quit Eitilt and were fighting to defend themselves on a personal level. The smoke and the cold also retreated. Yet Saeryn was not satisfied by this. She moved back to stand in the middle of her people and once there she threw her arms up into the air and began to radiate warm and rejuvenating light, as golden as the morning sun. As she did so, Andie and the dragonborn began to fill with energy, power. Saeryn was sacrificing her own power to refuel her people.

"Protect the Queen at all costs!" Andie yelled.

Some of the dragonborn warriors formed a tight circle around Saeryn to shield her from any attack. Before long all the civilians were fighting alongside the dragonborn, finally convinced of their innocence. The front of the University had turned into an all-out warzone—makeshift weapons had appeared and people were fighting in brutal hand-to-hand combat— and more members of the battalion were coming up from the University. Andie knew what to do then.

"Call the dragons!" she cried.

As one the warriors each called their specific call and then they all waited for the dragons to swoop down and bring the terrible fire. But when the dragons didn't show, they began to get worried. Andie made her way through the pandemonium to the edge of the crowd and looked to the mountainside where they had left the dragons. She couldn't believe her eyes.

The dragons were under attack. It was the Sentinels. Andie had completely forgotten their existence. The Sentinels were racing back and forth over the terrain, slashing and morphing and pounding almost too quickly to be seen. The dragons spit their fire as ferociously as they could, but the Sentinels moved too well to be hit by such passionate attacks.

The silver beings liquified and launched attacks that couldn't even be quantified. Andie and the dragonborn had been so preoccupied facing the threat they could see that they hadn't once looked back to make sure the dragons were okay. They had essentially abandoned them and played into the chancellor's plans once more. The riders who had been circling in the sky had gone down to help the dragons, but they had come under attack themselves. Andie wanted to go and help them, but there wasn't much she could do. She remembered what a threat the Sentinels could be, but she also knew that dragons were terrible foes to pick a fight with. They would have to care for themselves for the moment.

"The dragons are facing their own attack," she called when she got back to the center of the circle. "We'll have to do this on our own."

But just as she was about to relaunch the attack, she caught sight of Chancellor Mharú. He was lifting his hands into the air.

"I've anticipated every course of events," he said, grinning maliciously. "And I've been practicing this spell for almost forty years. Normally one needs a network of other sorcerers to help power the spell, but in special circumstances, much like this one, sacrifice works just as well."

The blue light began to emanate from his hands and in a matter of moments the tear had reopened in the sky.

The battalion closed ranks in front of the chancellor to protect him. Almost as soon as he began the spell, civilians began to drop all around. Andie raced to the nearest one and tried to save them, but their veins had already turned a dark blue and their skin was going loose on their body. Dead before they hit the ground. They were dropping in groves.

The dragonborn and the battalion all seemed fine. The spell must have been feeding on the energy of the weakest among them. Andie stood and began casting in the direction of the chancellor, but she couldn't even get close to him. And his spell was growing rapidly.

"You know the greatest thing about being a coward?" the chancellor called. "You're afraid of everything. And so, you plan and you scheme and you get really good at being clever. Before you know it, you're a master manipulator who has plans, and backup plans, and backups for the backups, and so on. Would you like to know what I'm talking about?"

"I'd like you to stop talking and come down here to face me," Andie called, never stopping her attack. "I see you've surrounded yourself with super soldiers and innocent people. Anything to avoid the fight."

"Obviously. I am afraid, after all. Try to keep up. Watch the next phase of my plan. Remember that psychic link I was talking about earlier, with your friend—sorry, dead friend—Marvo? I've been practicing on it for months. And once I have one person I can move from conscience to conscience. But why don't I just show you?"

The doors of the University opened and as more of the battalion began to come out Andie switched sides again and had her hand raised to cast a particularly nasty spell, but she stopped herself. She looked closer. It wasn't more members of the battalion coming through the doors. It was more civilians. They walked in a brisk, uniform way, not looking at anything in particular, just staring straight ahead. Andie knew instantly what the chancellor was planning. She turned to the dragonborn.

"We have to stop those people," she shouted. "He's luring them out here so that he can sacrifice them as fuel for his spell, we have to stop him."

The dragonborn began to cast on two fronts: one an offensive, fighting back the battalion and their invulnerable armor, the other a defensive, casting sleeping spells at the waves upon waves of people flowing out of the University's doors. Fortunately, the people were moving slowly enough that the dragonborn had soon stopped the flow and Andie collapsed the doorway so that no more could come out. She looked back at the chancellor, feeling victorious, but was surprised to see he was still smiling. More than that, he was laughing.

"You still don't understand, do you?" he asked, unbuttoning his shirt. "I don't need them to be awake. And as for the ones inside, I may not be able to see them, but the connection is already there. Look again."

Andie turned and saw that all the bodies they had put to sleep were already dead. The dark blue veins. The loose skin. It was a massacre. Chancellor Mharú's evil laughter made Andie turn around again. he had fully undressed and now she could see that he had been wearing the new armor under his suit.

"Now you should begin to understand," he said. "There is nothing you can do to stop this spell. I may not have the power to kill your precious dragonborn, but I can send them to a place that will do the killing for me. Which reminds me... my spell needs more power."

With those words the chancellor ran for the train, which Andie hadn't noticed was already beginning to move. A handful of the battalion followed him, including Ashur. Andie turned to ask for help, but with the insane number of battalion members, the space-time tear beginning to pull on all the dragonborn, and the dragons fighting for their lives against the Sentinels, she knew she couldn't take anyone with her. Even Saeryn was busy providing the energy of the sun. But the chancellor couldn't be allowed to get away—there was no telling how many lives he would take if he reached the bottom.

She turned and ran for the train. It was almost out of reach and she had to push herself to run faster than she ever had before. As the train slipped over the precipice and began its vertical descent, Andie leapt off the mountain after it.

CHAPTER NINETEEN

SHE WAS FALLING WITHOUT ANYTHING TO HOLD ON TO.
She was directly behind the train, but it was quickly
picking up speed and was pulling away from her. She
struggled and kicked, trying to maintain her focus, her
orientation, but she was freefalling and the train was
quickly escaping.

She stretched her hands out in front of her and
with her magic she pulled at the back of the train. The
entire back ten feet of the final car ripped off and
splintered into a thousand pieces. The largest parts of
the debris missed her, but some of the smaller pieces
cut her badly. But she was still trailing the train. She
used her magic to give her a violent forward push, and
she shot right down into the car.

But the gravity component was damaged because
of the loss of the back part of the car. She caught

herself on a sconce and began crawling down using whatever she could grab. All around her objects in the train were being ripped out of the car by speed and suction. She had to duck more than once to avoid being hit. When she finally reached the door, she grabbed the handle and settled her feet on the sides of the door.

When she turned the handle and opened it, half of the objects in the next room came rushing up. She evaded them and then flipped herself around to the other side of the door, closing it with a desperate slam. She was quick getting back to her feet: she'd gotten a good view of the room and knew there were at least two soldiers in it. As soon as the door closed, the gravity corrected and Andie leapt up. With a deft wave of her hand, she blew two of the soldiers out of the windows. But there were still six more, Ashur, and the chancellor.

"You know the best part of the spell, Andie?" Chancellor Mharú said. "As long as you can avoid being attacked yourself, you don't even have to stay with it for it to keep going. That spell will keep building and when I reach the city at the bottom of this mountain I'm going to find all the fuel I need. All I need to do is put myself around life and the spell will do the rest."

Andie glared at the man before her. "You talk too much."

She cast right at his face but it was blocked by the battalion. The chancellor and Ashur raced into the next car. They were followed by all except two soldiers. Andie didn't have time for anymore pleasantries.

"Saeryn, forgive me."

Andie channeled her power into a ball of black fire so hot and so powerful that it melted one of the soldier's armor. Her magic always amazed her, and even still, she hardly believed she was capable of the things she had managed these past few months. She stared after the black fire with wide eyes, a strange mix of sorcerer's and dragonborn magic. Her own strange brand of whatever it was. She wasn't exactly sure what to call it, apart from terrifying.

She tried to ignore the screams as the suit melted onto his skin and he collapsed. Not dead, but certainly wishing he was. She swallowed back the bile that crept up her throat at the smell of burning flesh as she pressed forward. She couldn't allow herself to be affected by such thing. Not when the survival of her entire race and the entire city of Arvall relied on her succeeding at her task.

The other soldier began a panicked attack that betrayed his fear and Andie easily avoided his incompetent display. She began to swirl her hand around and around, focusing her energy on the soldier. Soon a vortex began to gather behind him and in a matter of moments he had been lifted and was spinning and tumbling out of control.

Andie spun her hand faster and faster until the vortex was a miniscule tornado, whipping everything in sight into a fury. She flung the soldier and the tornado over her shoulder and the man hit the back wall so hard Andie heard his spine crack. She'd never wanted violence, not really. But if trouble was what they wanted she was going to give them as much as they could handle.

As she burst into the next car, the group of villains was just moving through the door at the other end. She cast a bolt of lightning and hit one of the soldiers, but only succeeded in knocking him into the next room and closing the door. She rushed across the car and flung open the door. The man she'd hit was already up and running. She chased him down easily, as his wound was slowing him, and at the same instant her hand met his back she sent her magic into him, paralyzing him totally. He hit the floor and Andie never stopped moving.

In the next car, the first thing she did was throw a wall of magic. All the furniture, fixtures, appliances, and other objects in the room were hurled forward ahead of the chancellor. The great field of debris collided with the door and totally blocked off the escape. But the chancellor was quick on his feet. He spied an emergency ladder leading to the roof and he and Ashur quickly went up and out, followed by three of the soldiers. That left two soldiers she hadn't seen before, obviously already stationed on the train.

Her spell with the furniture had broken all the lights in the car and so, with the exception of the moonlight and other sources flashing by outside, the car was totally dark. In fact, all Andie could see were two glowing pairs of hand. They began casting immediately, terrible and deadly spells that only served to further remind Andie how ruthless the University was. Her advantages were the dark and her ability to stay calm when her opponents were clearly frantic.

She used her stealth to close the distance in the dark and then cast a low spell at one of the soldiers' legs. He leapt to his left to avoid it and landed right where she wanted him. She got in close and took him with hand-to-hand. During their months in the tunnel, Marvo and Raesh had taught her much. The soldier was stronger and faster because of his armor, but Andie had the better training. She laid him out flat in less than two minutes. When she turned to the other soldier, he crouched down and threw up his hands in surrender.

She rushed past him and jumped on the ladder, but just as she was about to climb up to the roof, the soldier grabbed her. Unfortunately for him, she'd figured it was a trick. In one deft movement, she kicked him off and threw herself up on the roof. As soon as he stuck his head up through the hole, Andie caught him with a hook in the center of his face. He went crashing back down.

She was using her magic to hold herself upright, but with the incredible speed of the train it was a difficult job. Not to mention the train was traveling vertically at that point. She started walking forward and could already see the chancellor and his battalion ahead. As soon as she stepped onto the next car, she disconnected all the ones behind her and the train soon left them behind.

"You're very good," the chancellor called through the night. "If only you weren't dragonborn, and fought for me. Ah well. Disappointment abounds."

"Why?" she screamed through the violent wind that lashed her hair across her face. The roar of the train flying through the cold air muffled her cries. "What possible good will come of all this bloodshed? They'll never accept you now, never give you the power you want so badly. You've killed so many people, and for what? To keep spreading a lie?"

"I want what all men with power want, Andie. More power. You are part of the new generation that wants nothing, does nothing, is satisfied with sand when you could have diamonds. But not me. I'll never stop, I'll never have enough."

"It's power you don't need! You're the chancellor

of western Noelle. Half of this entire continent is under your control. Why can't you—"

"The world has lost its way! We've stopped trying, stopped striving! I want it all! Everything!"

He and Ashur continued on, leaving the final three battalion soldiers in Andie's path. She looked around and saw that they were nearing the end of the line. Soon the chancellor would be in the city and if he made it that far there would be no stopping him. The three soldiers looked skittish as Andie approached, no doubt wary of her power now after seeing her plow through all their friends.

Andie stopped, eyed them fiercely. "This man is on his way to suck the life out of Arvall. That means that in a matter of minutes everything and everyone you know will be gone. They will be dead. Your friends, your family. All of them."

They froze in place as they listened to her speak. She took it as a sign to continue.

"You don't need to do this. You owe him nothing," she pleaded. "Are you really going to stand between him and me? Your lives are worth more than this."

The soldiers looked at each other and even with their faces covered, Andie could tell they were reconsidering. She took another step forward and they took one back. One of them removed his mask and relaxed his battle stance.

"We're not from around here," he yelled over the

sound of the rushing wind. "None of the battalion is. We don't know these people. They mean nothing to us."

"I'm not from around here, either. I'm from Michaelson, a small farming village near Gordric's Pain. But these people... they mean something to me. If the chancellor sees that he can only get his way by mass murder, how long do you think he'll stay calm? How long before it's your cities and your people that he's massacring? I'm going to stop him and I'm going to do it now. The only question is, do I take you down with him?"

The larger soldier looked at Andie and then back at his peers. They each nodded to him and he put his helmet back on and charged his suit. Andie clenched her fists and prepared to attack, but just as she raised her hands the soldier nodded to her, and he and his friends jumped from the train, covering themselves in bubbles of protective magic to break their fall. Andie let out a long breath she had been holding, turned her attention forward again, and carried on.

Tarven and the chancellor had reached the front of the train and run out of places to run or hide. Andie finally caught up with them and nearly had her head taken off by a white bolt of lightning thrown back by Ashur. The bolt missed her by an inch and hit the car behind her. It split the entire roof apart. He had come a long way since she last knew him.

Everything about him was different. His expressions, his body, his energy. She sensed he had done terrible things since the last time they saw each other. A lot of terrible things. What shocked her most was his power. Before, he had merely been talented with hortological magic, but now his speed, power, and casting ability were off the charts. Even better than his comrades. He must've been good, because he was the last line of defense between the chancellor and Andie, and the chancellor didn't look worried at all.

"You truly are a marvelous thing, Andie Rogers," Chancellor Mharú called. "I've never seen anything like you. Well, almost never," he said, patting Ashur's shoulder.

Andie couldn't help but roll her eyes. "You'll have to do better than that to impress me, I'm afraid, Chancellor."

He ignored her. "I'm feeling rather ecstatic, and so I'll offer you your life this one time. Join me. Come over to my side and see what real power feels like. Touch it, possess it, relish it. If you were ever to put on this armor there would be nothing on this earth that could stop you."

"Are you out of your mind? You're trying to eradicate my people! You killed my friends, tried to kill my father, and have proven yourself to be nothing but pure evil."

"Those are just people, Andie, and the world is full of them. Find a new home, adopt a new culture, reinvent yourself. Take the things you want. Don't let anything stand in your way."

"Take," she repeated, beginning to almost glow with rage. "Take. Like you took my mother?"

"Fine, Andie. You want to be a martyr, then let us help you die."

Ashur began moving forward toward her. The train began to gradually level out as they neared the bottom of the mountain. This time, Andie cast first and although her aim was perfect, it only caused Ashur to stumble a little.

He retaliated with a spell that wrapped her in super-cold air, and she had to catch her breath quickly in order to defend against his next attack. He cast again, but she caught it and flung it back at him, bringing him to his knees. As he stood again, he conjured a long chain in his hands, but instead of steel, each link was made of freezing energy. He lashed out and missed her twice, but the third time the chain wrapped around her arm and caught her, and the pain was so intense she wanted to scream.

Ashur pulled on the chain and the armor gave him such strength that Andie was pulled off her feet. As soon as her feet left the train, Andie flew up and away. The train was still traveling at an incredible speed. The only thing that kept her from flying away was the chain wrapped around her arm. Using her magic, she cut the chain and brought herself back to the roof. But before she could stand, Ashur lashed out with the chain again and this time it wrapped around her body, pinning down one of her arms. She steadied herself, but the freezing cold was draining the energy right out of her. Ashur was strong, so much more powerful than she'd imagined.

But she couldn't fail. She accessed a deeper part of her magic and released it, engulfing herself in flames and melting the chain right off. Ashur lashed out again, but Andie burned so hot the chain evaporated before it reached her. She almost melted through the roof. When Ashur discarded the chain, Andie returned to her normal state and cast a flurry of spells at Ashur that even his armor couldn't block or absorb. When they hit, she heard his arm and his ribs break.

She had assumed the fight was over and began walking past him to get to the chancellor. The train levelled out completely as it began to slow and pull into the station. Andie was only a few steps from the chancellor when a hand grabbed her and flung her back twenty feet. She very nearly slid off the train entirely. Ashur was back on his feet and moving his arm as if nothing had happened. Andie couldn't believe it.

"That's impossible," she said. "I heard the bones break."

"Did you really think the University wouldn't figure it out?" he asked. "They've been experimenting on people with dragon's blood for years. They finally figured out how to mimic your healing abilities. This suit will never work as well as an actual dragonborn body, it's a lot slower and can't heal completely, but it does the trick. You can't win, Andie."

"I have to."

"Then you'll die trying."

"This isn't you, Tarven."

Tarven glared at her, a fiery light illuminating his piercing gaze. "Tarven is dead. My name is Ashur."

CHAPTER TWENTY

ANDIE COULDN'T BELIEVE WHAT SHE WAS HEARING. She cried out and shook her head, her eyes clouded with angry tears that threatened to spill from her lids. Tear of rage. "No, you're wrong. Your name is Tarven and this isn't you! I know you wanted to impress them, to be accepted by them, but I can't honestly believe you're this evil. Think about what's happening around you. He's about to go into your city and take innocent lives. Are you honestly okay with that?"

"I am completely loyal to him. I swore my allegiance and I will do nothing, *nothing*, to jeopardize the work that he is doing. He is building an empire greater than anything you can imagine. A continental kingdom governed by a single, infallible power. And he chose me to lead his battalion, and, one day, all of his legions. The future is now, Andie. The future is Myamar Mharú."

"What happened to that boy who tested me my first day at the University? That cocky, but sweet boy who spent all those afternoons teaching me, helping me, showing me magic I'd never even dreamed of? Where is he? All he wanted was to show the world how special his plants were. What happened to him?"

Ashur was silent then. He seemed to be trying to think of a suitable response, but couldn't. Something about his expression then made Andie pause; she couldn't quite tell what was happening inside of him, but the expression on his face was almost one of regret. She thought then, seriously, that he might not truly be loyal to the chancellor, or the University, or any of it. He might be just as trapped and threatened as Lilja was. He might just be another pawn in the chancellor's vast and ever adapting game.

But Ashur clenched his fists and the suit began to glow, and Andie knew that either he was too brainwashed to stop himself or he truly had gone over the edge of reason. He flung another bolt of lightning at her, this time grazing her side. Behind him, Chancellor Mharú was jumping onto the platform, as the train had almost completely stopped moving. They'd arrived at the station.

"So, you want to trade lighting?" Andie asked. "Let's see what you can do."

Ashur cast another white bolt and Andie met it in the air with a black one. And back and forth they traded lightning, black and white, hot and cold, like a miniature copy of the Hot Salts of Mithraldia. Ashur was well trained, methodical, precise. Andie was organic, intuitive, powerful. The bolts flashed through the air with a terrible sound as loud as any real lightning in the sky. As the bolts sailed by, they hit the train, the platform, various parts of the station, and anything else in their path. Andie and Ashur were destroying everything around them. Andie looked for the chancellor, but he was already gone. She needed to move, fast.

Ashur reached back to conjure his next bolt and Andie did that thing she only did in times of great distress: she reached into the deepest reaches of her magic and released it. A black bolt of lightning erupted from her chest and shot out with such force that she slid back on the train. The bolt was so wide it seemed more like a stream of energy that was wrapped in violent purple flames. Ashur was blown away so hard and fast that Andie couldn't see where he landed or if he was even still alive. She leapt off the train and ran to find the chancellor.

She cleared the station and was running down the nearest boulevard when she stopped. She had no idea where he'd gone. The city was huge, sprawling, and he'd gotten a considerable head start and could have been anywhere by then.

Andie wracked her brain trying to think where he could go to get the quickest access to a large, dense population, but there was no end to the possibilities. The arena, the pier, any of the six boulevards in the publishing district, the financial district, the baseball stadium— Andie could hear them cheering from the train station— and on and on. She was at a total loss. For all she knew he had already started his mass sacrifice. She looked up toward the mountain and saw a tiny dot of light that was almost invisible from so far away. The tear. It had grown.

Just as Andie was about to lose her mind, the screaming began. She turned and began running toward the sounds. She could hear cars crashing and explosions as complete and utter chaos spread in the distance. She ran as fast as she can, wishing the entire time that she had a dragon who cut the air and have her in the area to save people. The closer she got, the more she heard, the more she feared, the more she pushed herself to run faster and harder. When she finally reached the intersection where everything was happening she was met by two things: fear and death.

There were bodies everywhere. There were far too many to count and even the people running were tripping over the corpses that littered the road in every direction. Even as she looked up at the buildings,

Andie could see bodies collapsed in the windows. As the people ran, fled, they were killed in midstride. Andie turned and turned, trying to find any sign of hope or salvation, but there was nothing there except carnage and sheer terror.

The chancellor was moving down the street ahead of her. He was standing on a section of the pavement that he had ripped up and it was floating him along at an increasing speed. Andie began chasing him, but he was moving too fast. She could hear him laughing as the bodies continued to fall all around him. As he turned to watch the destruction, he saw her.

"You simply won't die, will you?" he asked. "No matter, the spell is already begun. It's self-sustaining now. All I have to do is wait."

"You're killing the entire city! This is madness! Please, stop!"

"It's too late for your pleas, little girl. Although, if it makes you feel any better I was never going to stop. The plan was always to get rid of the dragonborn by sacrificing the city and then blame the mass destruction on your people. Then the world would be in a constant state of fear, hiding from a threat that didn't even exist."

"That's sick," Andie managed to spit out.

The chancellor laughed suddenly. "No, brilliant I think is the correct word."

"You're only—"

"Stop trying to reason with me, girl."

The chancellor turned and began floating even faster. Andie stopped running. There was no way she could keep up with him on foot. Again, she wished for a dragon. Then she remembered a conversation she'd had with Saeryn. She'd told Saeryn about that night in the archives when, for a few moments, she'd levitated while fighting against the University. Saeryn had told her that it was possible for a dragonborn to levitate and even fly if they had the power, the concentration, and the will. She said it was a rare and powerful trait.

Andie had practiced some on the mountain without much luck, but now she was out of options and the dragons were too far away. She closed her eyes and went to that deep recess of herself, where her most incredible power resided. She focused all her energy, all her power. She tried to picture in her mind what she wanted to do, but although she felt the power she didn't feel the change.

Yet when she finally gave up and opened her eyes, much to her surprise she found she was hovering. When she blinked and refocused her eyes, she noticed she was actually at least five feet above the ground. It had worked. She couldn't believe it. For a split second, she allowed herself to laugh. A nervous sound that erupted from her lips, so foreign after the darkness she's endured these past months. But her momentary thrill caught her off-guard and she slipped suddenly from the air. Fortunately, her will and determination froze her in mid fall and she propelled herself back up, an air of defiance on her face.

She steadied her hands beside her and began to will herself forward. It took a tremendous amount of concentration, but she found herself flying toward the chancellor, moving faster and faster. He was so busy enjoying the sight of the bodies falling that he almost missed her, but when he did see her flying toward him, a change came over him. For the first time that night, Andie could see that he was afraid. The sight of a powerful dragonborn flying toward him with only one goal in mind terrified him. He cast more magic at his pavement and the chase began.

They weaved through the streets of the city, moving faster and faster. Andie had some issues controlling her flight and she more than once knocked against buildings and lamp posts. The chancellor was so busy trying to escape that he stopped looking back, refused to see the girl coming for him. For her part, Andie was as exhilarated as she was afraid.

Time was running out and as they weaved in and out and between and around she was aware that the spell was spreading at an incredible rate. The magic followed the chancellor, but it also spread out from wherever it landed. The more Andie chased him, the more she helped him spread his poison. And, of course, she never forgot that her people were back up on Brie, fighting for their lives and the culture of their entire people. The dragons, too, were locked in battle to the death. And the innocent civilians of Arvall were the collateral damage of a senseless and profitless war.

There was no time. Everywhere around her was death and screams and fear. The chancellor had created something so terrible Andie's heart was breaking more and more each second. She thought of the millions of people dying across the city. She thought of her people dying, perhaps already dead, on Brie. She thought her friends, the fighters, wounded and broken in spirit thousands of leagues away. Marvo. Carmen. Her father. Her entire world. Enough was enough.

She pushed herself like she had never done before and soared forward so rapidly she closed the distance between herself and the chancellor in less than a second. She collided with him, taking him off his floating ground and through the window of a skyscraper they were passing. The crashed through the glass and tumbled across the tiled floor, hitting the ground so hard they lost their breath. By the time Andie looked up, the magic had killed everyone on the floor and she was sure the magic was spreading up through the building as she stood there. In fact, the magic had grown so strong and so vast that even Andie was beginning to feel the effects; she simply hadn't noticed before. The chancellor looked as though he were still having trouble catching his breath as he rolled over on his side and pulled a large piece of glass from the side of his face. As the blood ran down over his mouth he looked up at Andie, smiling.

"Well, even I couldn't plan for this," he said, undaunted. "I didn't know you could fly."

"I can do a lot of things. Including showing you what real pain feels like if you don't stop this spell."

"Oh, I think it's too late for that. Look around you, the spell can't be stopped. Most of the city is already dead and soon the rest will be, too. Lucky for you, you're nowhere near the gateway to the past. I would have loved to watch you be sucked away."

"It is not too late. You can still save whoever's left. You can put a stop to this!"

"You mistake me for someone who cares about these people, girl."

"How can one person be so evil? What is wrong with you?"

"Me? I just wanted power. Respect. I wanted to walk out in the sun and not be thought a coward. And now I've failed. I think I've performed the spell incorrectly. Look…"

The chancellor held up his hand and Andie saw that the veins were beginning to turn dark blue. The skin was dying, beginning to wither even as she watched.

"You're dying," she said, in disbelief. "No! Who's going to stop the spell?"

He began laughing manically then. "Oh, stupid girl. It's not the spell you should be worried about, but our one greatest weapon that I leave behind."

"Weapon, what weapon?" Andie pleaded, falling to her knees. "What can possibly be worse than killing an entire city?"

Mharú tried to push himself up from the ground, but he immediately fell back, his body too weak to even lift his head. "This spell is tied to me. I'm dying, but there the true power still lives." His laugh transformed into an eerie cackle that made Andie take another step back from him. "He lives. And so long as he lives, so long as the weapon is alive—and I promise you, girl, that suit of his will keep him alive —the world has no hope. You think me killing a city is bad, just you wait until you see the destruction my Ashur can do."

Andie shook her head in disbelief. "You're a fool if you think Tarven will carry on your evil plan for you. Besides, I don't think he's even still al—"

"Stupid girl," the chancellor snapped, bloody spittle spraying before him as he spoke. "You're missing the point. It's not about the spell. It will stop when I die, which seems to be any moment now." More red spilled across the floor as he rolled to his side and coughed up more blood.

Andie stood frozen, staring down at the man before her. She had never wanted to kill anyone so badly in her life, but there he lay, dying before her. Part of her was grateful she wouldn't be forced to let Saeryn down by becoming a murderer. Another part of her was angry that he took that task away from her.

"You know I never hated your people. Not really. Not until tonight. When I woke up this morning the whole world was soon to be mine. And now I'm dying by my own hand and the only person here to say goodbye is a girl I tried to kill."

"Don't do this. Don't let it end like this. Do the right thing, please."

His voice was barely a whisper, his breaths coming in slow, gurgling wheezes. With one final effort, he looked up at her and spoke. "You'll never understand the allure of power, little girl. But no matter. You lost, anyway."

With that, the chancellor laid his head back on the floor and clenched his fists. The suit began to charge and glow. Andie took several uncertain steps back before she realized what he was doing. He was going to give the spell one last wave of magic to sustain it. Enough to kill anyone left in the city. She dove for his body, her hands outstretched before her, but she was too late.

Chancellor Myamar exploded right before her and she was met in midair by a wave of magic unlike anything she'd ever experienced. The armor had amplified his final spell immensely. Andie was thrown back out toward the street and across it, until she crashed through the window of the next building and collided with the floor. The last thing she saw was the wave of blue magic traveling out across the city and the building where she'd been thrown from collapsing in an unbelievable cloud of smoke, debris, and noise.

HE WAS JARRED awake from the unbelievable pain. It felt as if his entire body were burning and as he looked down at himself, or what was left of him, he nearly fainted from the shock.

One of his hands was gone, as was most of his arm below the elbow. His legs were so badly burned they were undistinguishable as legs and one of them was totally numb and wouldn't move. Every time he twisted his body, the discs in his back grinded against each other. Both his arms were in excruciating pain. He lifted his remaining hand to feel his head and felt that not only was his hair completely burned off, but the skin of his face was totally melted. And he could only see out of one eye. He was so shocked and was in so much agony that he could hardly move.

The only thing that remained largely undamaged was his torso. As the leader of the battalion his uniform had a thicker, more advanced chest plate so that his suit could harness more energy and deliver a more powerful performance. The torso of his armor remained largely undamaged and was the only thing that had saved his life.

The enormous bolt of black lightning that Andie had used against him had thrown him over two hundred feet away. It took him quite some time to comprehend his world through the pain and figure out where he was. He looked into the sky and saw the blue wave of magic. Chancellor Myamar Mharú's final desperate act. The man he'd sworn his allegiance and life to was gone, had failed.

He rolled over onto the chest plate with a grunt of pain and began to crawl. He didn't make it very far before he stopped, in so much terrible agony that he wanted to cry, to give up and die right then and there. He had never known such pain, such desperation. His skin was peeling off on the ground as he crawled and his back, more than likely broken, felt like it was tearing apart.

He gathered his strength and continued. The pain grew worse the farther he went, but with his goal in mind he knew he could make it to a safe place, somewhere he could meet up with other members of the battalion and regroup. This was only the beginning. And though he was broken, burned, and defeated, he was not without his rage.

CHAPTER TWENTY-ONE

"How long will they stay like that?" Oren asked.

"As long as we need them to," Saeryn responded, looking at her work. "We gave them every chance we possibly could, Oren. There was nothing left but this."

When the final blast of magic had gone out from the chancellor, Saeryn had looked down on the city as its entire population was wiped out in one, maleficent move. Her heart had broken to see such unadulterated evil and she grew tired of it. She grew weary of battle and destruction. She ended her spell of light and went to face the battalion. As they converged on her, she rose into the air and began to revolve, sweeping her arms all around her, casting a spell that even the University's armor couldn't withstand. By the time she came back to the ground, the entire battalion was frozen still—those near her, those in the University, even the ones spread out around the mountain. Her spell was that powerful.

"What about the tear?" Oren asked. "It has closed for now, but how do we know it won't be back? We have to find the chancellor and stop him."

"Andie went after him," Saeryn said. "And I'm afraid she caught up with him."

"What do you mean?"

"That wave of magic. It had to be the chancellor. And even with his new armor there is no way a sorcerer could survive an expense of magic like that. He is surely dead. Even the Sentinels have ceased to attack and they would only stop if their commander were defeated. I fear what Andie may have done when she caught him. She may have... perhaps..."

"No," Oren said, his voice filling with fear and doubt and other things. "I know I don't know her as well as you do, but I've spent some time with her and I don't think... I know she's not capable of something like this. Not Andie. She couldn't. She wouldn't."

"I don't wish to consider it either, Oren, but what else is there? What other explanation? The chancellor would not have gone through all this effort and scheming simply to take his own life. What would you have me believe?"

"I say we should give her the benefit of the doubt. Wait for her return and ask her. Whatever happened, she would not lie to us. But she couldn't kill. Not Andie."

"Regardless, we have more pressing things to attend to. Look at all this carnage."

As she spoke, she indicated all the bodies lying around the entrance of the University and throughout the lot and the precipice. All the bodies were darkly veined and the skin hung loose on the corpses. There were hundreds of them on the mountain alone and Saeryn knew that with that blast of radical, unmonitored magic from the chancellor every soul in the city would be dead. Millions of people sacrificed to feed an all-consuming spell that had ultimately failed. Not a single dragonborn warrior or dragon had been taken up into the tear. The chancellor's grand design had failed. And all the wounds and breaks the dragonborn had sustained were already beginning to heal. The dragons, too, were improving with each second—only three of them had sustained serious injuries, but they would be healed within the hour.

Saeryn and Oren walked toward the precipice and looked down toward the city, thinking of all the bodies that must have littered the streets, buildings, stations, boulevards, parks, and every other space. Bodies killed in midstride or in the middle of eating. Bodies sucked dry of all vitality while they slept or woke. Bodies silenced and broken forever without ever having done anything to deserve their end. Saeryn hid her face in her hands, momentarily overcome by the unbelievable sadness. Like Andie before her, she couldn't believe or understand how anyone could be so evil, so careless with the lives of millions of people they had claimed to protect. Oren rested a hand on her shoulder. And for a moment they just stood there.

Sometime later, when Saeryn had composed herself, she decided on a plan of action. She understood that life had a balance, that once certain events took place they couldn't be erased or altered. Or at least they shouldn't be. There was a course to things, a flow and current of life and death and everything in between that went on its way unobstructed, and Saeryn knew that that was simply the way things were. But suddenly that wasn't good enough for her anymore. Not then. Not that night of all nights. Time and death were very dangerous things to toy with, whether one was skilled in magic or not, and there were rules and structures to the handling of each. Saeryn was prepared to break one of the highest of those rules.

"Oren, I need your help and the help of our people. It is not right that all these people should die for us. They came here tonight with one goal in heart and by the time they were brutally murdered they had come to see the error of their ways. And even if they hadn't, it isn't right to leave them here like this, broken and forlorn. I want to save them. I want to do what only our people can. It will be harder without the rest of our people here, but we can draw on the University's battalion for strength. What say you, Oren? Can your Queen count on you?"

"You can always count on me, Saeryn. But, what do you intend to do?" He glanced out at the broken and scattered bodies, uncertain at what she was implying.

"I intend to bring them back."

Oren's eyes grew wide as he stared at his Queen. "But that's impossible. You know we don't have the power to return people to life."

"Perhaps not, but I would rather die than not at least try."

Blinking rapidly, Oren finally bowed. "Of course. I cannot think of one thing I wish more than to return these people back their lives, though I'm afraid my reasons pale in their honor next to yours. I was thinking that they were the only people on the face of this planet who could tell the whole world that we weren't evil. They saw with their own eyes how evil and callous the chancellor and his men were. I will round up our people."

Oren went off to apprise his fellow dragonborn of what Saeryn wanted to do and gather them for the event. Saeryn directed some of the men to bring the unconscious battalion members to a central location to create a point of focus. Once these tasks were all complete, the dragonborn kneeled around the bodies of the frozen battalion members and then bowed their heads. They began to link with one another, holding hands and placing hands on shoulders. Saeryn began the spell and each of the dragonborn warriors picked it up until they were all chanting in unison. She knew there was hardly a chance in the world the spell would work, but given the dark and evil nature of the people's slaughter, she knew she at least had to try.

The chanting grew louder as the dragonborn worked as one. Their efforts appeared for naught, though, as hardly a glimmer of life returned to the people. But then something incredibly happened. The dragons had finally rejoined their riders and they lay down next to the group, encircling the dragonborn and lending strength and comfort. The magic amplified, a new and strange energy washing over the city. One so strong and so new that Saeryn hardly believed what she was feeling. She closed her eyes and let it consume her, offering her very being to aid the spell.

The mountain went still, quiet as the night sky. It had already become eerily calm after the unspeakable massacre, but this was new, unique. The spell had stopped all motion and sound on the mountain, and had even stopped motion and sound in the city below. All of Arvall, for the first time since its conception, was in a state of peace. The dragons inched closer to the dragonborn and nuzzled their backs.

The dragons' eyes began to shimmer and then the iridescent skin around the eyes began to shift through innumerable pearlescent shades of color that had no name. This was something the dragons hadn't done in a very long time. In fact, none of the living dragonborn had ever seen it, not even Saeryn. Their eyes began to behave that way when the dragons needed to provide the strength and magic a dragonborn needed to save a life. It was an ancient magic, one long lost to history. One Saeryn had thought lost forever.

They worked as one until nearly all their magic had depleted, but it was not enough. Saeryn could feel the magic wane. She squeezed her eyes shut and willed every fiber of her being into the spell, drawing on the ancient magic of her royal house, pushing as much of that energy out into the souls of the people around her. But it wasn't until Raylim—beautiful, strong, and selfless Raylim—flew down before Saeryn and cast his own life's energy out into the world, that the spell finally took. With one final effort, Raylim raised his silver head high up to the sky and let out a powerful breath of fire. The flames flew so high, they penetrated the clouds. For a moment, the entire city glowed in Raylim's warm light, and then the dragon softly laid down his head and gave his life to save those around him.

Saeryn held onto the spell, gazing down at the

creature who had just sacrificed himself for the cause. Tears streamed down her face as she harnessed the last magical energy that emanated from his body, letting the heat from his flames fuel her magic, and blasted it out over the city streets. A silver, beautiful magic that offered exactly what was necessary for the spell to succeed. Saeryn fell to her knees and wept. "Thank you, my friend."

Not many minutes had passed before the first sign of the spell's efficiency appeared. Saeryn didn't believe her eyes at first, convinced her vision was deceiving her. She blinked through her tears to clear her eyes. She saw a man lying dead near the dragonborn begin to change. The dark blue color in his veins receded. His loose skin tightened on his corpse. Before long, his fingers started to move and not long after that the man was on his feet, confused but alive. He was soon followed by a woman and then another man, and before long there were bodies rising all around them.

Inside the University, the people that the chancellor had tricked into coming there to sacrifice themselves began to wake and roll off each other. They had a vague recollection of having a voice inside their heads asking them to come up to the University and to go along with whatever happened there. As they began to wander out into the night they saw the dragonborn and the dragons, kneeling in a circle and chanting in a beautiful, solemn rhythm.

Below the mountain, in the city itself, the people began to live. They revived in the exact positions they had died in, sometimes with a cough or a gasp. They couldn't believe it. The last thing they'd known they were having all the life and memories sucked out of their bodies; they remembered feeling cold, then numb, then nothing. But now they were back again, standing on their feet and breathing the sweet, clean air. They began to cheer and pray and cry tears of joy for being back, for being saved. And they knew exactly who had saved them.

Everyone had seen Chancellor Mharú floating through the streets and spreading that horrible magic everywhere. They remember his cruel smile and the way he enjoyed watching them perish. Some of them had lived long enough to see that final wave of magic as it rushed for them and took their lives. They had no doubt about who had done this to them and because of that they began to rethink everything they had feared, thought, rejected, accepted, and wanted. They also knew who to thank for their salvation. Saeryn wasn't just casting a spell, she was broadcasting a message. She was sending a telepathic message to everyone in the city telling them exactly what had happened and letting them know that there were witnesses to prove it—witnesses who had come to the top of the mountain to see the dragonborn dead, but then found themselves fighting beside them.

Even with the strength of the dragons and the battalion members, the dragonborn began to grow weak. It was a massive spell and the amount of power and skill it took were tremendous. As the final slain civilians came back to life, Saeryn and the dragonborn let go of each other and sat down to relax. It was the largest, most taxing spell any of them had ever done, though it would have been so much easier if they had all their people, even the children, helping. The dragons were the last to quiet, each laying its head on the floor in exhaustion. They had spent every ounce of their magical energy, but it had worked. Their magic had saved the city.

The civilians began to close in around them and one man stepped forward from the rest. "You saved us," he said, stunned, trembling. "I can't believe it. We were so wrong about you, about all of you."

"It was not I, but the combined efforts of my people and our dragons," Saeryn replied, pushing herself from her knees. "Raylim here, in particular. He sacrificed himself so you can live."

The man gaped down at still form of the massive dragon.

"Such a beautiful creature." Tears welled in the man's eyes. "I have never seen such a thing. To think,

I believed them evil my entire life. Such lies, such evil. We almost went along with that lunatic."

"He was a cruel, manipulative man," Saeryn replied. "I fault you not for believing what had been told as truth for so long. But he is gone now and he can no longer hurt anyone. The real truth is now clear, as you can now see. I see no reason for us to be enemies."

"I'm so embarrassed. I think we all are. We almost agreed to wipe out you and your entire people, and all because we listened to a man we started out not trusting in the first place. I guess we were desperate. Afraid. Can you ever forgive us?"

"There is nothing to forgive, my friend," she said, rising to her feet, although she was still incredibly tired. "He tricked you. And although you all did make the decision for yourselves to believe him, I would never hold a grudge against you for acting out of fear. It happens to the best of us. I would simply ask that we move forward in peace. I hope now you all understand that my people and I are not dangerous. We've found a place in the mountains, far away from here, and I can assure you that you will never see us again. We can be happy and whole there, leaving you to enjoy your homes and your lives in peace. You have my word that there is nothing to fear from us. We're not so very different. Our abilities may differ and our histories may have diverged, but we are all people, after all, and we all want the freedom to live and be happy."

The man turned to look at the other civilians and see what they thought. They all nodded vigorously, though they seemed sad. The man looked sad as well as he turned back to face Saeryn.

"What's your name?" he asked.

"My name is Saeryn."

"Queen of the dragonborn," Oren announced as he stepped forward.

"Well, your Grace, we have no intention of harming you or standing in your way, though you and your people have proven here tonight that even a small group of you is formidable. But I think it would be reckless of us to send you away to some distant mountain. Unless of course that's what you want."

"The dragonborn thrive in mountains," Saeryn said. "It would not be a punishment or a hardship. We would simply be going home."

"I see. Well, we won't ever spread these lies or this hate again. We'll never blindly follow another leader, either. We'll do better from now on. I promise. But... I wonder... if you might consider staying for a while? Or maybe visiting periodically? It's just that we've been so wrong for all our lives and I think I can speak for everyone else when I say that we'd like a chance to get to know the real dragonborn. We'd love to live with you and learn from you. Like you said, there's no reason for us to be enemies and if we're not enemies then perhaps we could be allies. We completely understand if you want to go or need to get back, but I want you to know that the door is open and we want you here. Also, this new world and its technology must be so foreign to you. They hadn't even discovered electricity yet in your time. And since you came through a portal here in our city, it's the responsibility of the citizens of Arvall to show you how to survive and thrive in this new world."

"You're genuine about wanting us around?" Saeryn asked, humbled by the man's kindness and soft-spoken way.

"More serious than I've ever been. We all are." Murmurs or agreement erupted around him, an endless stream of people approaching and thanking and crying their appreciation.

Saeryn looked up and around at all the people. They were all nodding their heads and smiling at her. All the dragonborn warriors gazed around themselves and met with smiles and handshakes and tears. The people had truly changed, had finally come to understand that it was never the dragonborn who had been evil or manipulative. It was never the dragonborn who had lied, murdered, stolen, and deceived every inch of the way just so that they could amass an invulnerable stockpile of power. It had been the University. It had *always* been the University. It wasn't long before the dragonborn themselves were beginning to smile and respond in kind. Saeryn's heart was filled to bursting with happiness and relief. She reached out her hands to the man and brought him closer to herself.

"Very well, then," she said. "We shall be allies."

A collective cheer went up from everyone there. Civilians, sorcerers, and dragonborn alike. They began to embrace each other and welcome each other. It was the most joy that any of them had experienced in a very long time. Saeryn looked all around her at the people celebrating and hugging each other. It was what she had always hoped for, but never expected to ever actually come to pass.

She was absolutely overwhelmed by the sheer and unfiltered mirth. But as she turned around and around she realized that there was someone missing. Someone who had worked as hard as she had and sacrificed even more so that they could be standing there on that precipice, arm-in-arm with their former enemies. Andie. She strode to the edge of the precipice and looked down over the city.

If anyone deserved to see the result of this hard and dangerous work, it was Andie.

"So, what happens next? By now they've reached

Arvall City and they've either managed to convince the people that they're not a threat or a lot of people are dead. What now?"

"Well, captain, the only thing we can do until they get back or until we get word is wait. The ship is completely destroyed and I don't think any of us is familiar with this area so if we start just walking there's no telling where we'll end up. Besides, too many of us are injured or unconscious. It would just be too much chaos to do anything now."

"I understand. And what about the bodies of all the ones we've lost? I didn't want to say anything in front of the group, but if those bodies are left out much longer the smell is really going to be a problem. We need to arrange a mass funeral. I know it's not the right way and I know it's not what any of us wants or deserves, but that's what we're going to do. It's dishonorable to leave them out like this. They sacrificed too much for the rest of us."

"You're right. Honestly, captain we should've buried them by now, but I just haven't had the will to face this yet."

"Raesh, I'm sorry about your father. I truly am. I've known Marvo since we were kids and he was one of my closest friends. I didn't hesitate for a second when he told me to be at the port and be ready to take him and his people to safety. He was only human and yet he was one of the bravest and strongest men I ever met. He died an honorable death, fighting for a cause that meant something to him. To all of us. He died a brave and honorable man."

Raesh sighed and offered a smile to the captain. "I know. He was a great man. I'm proud to have called him my father. It doesn't make this any easier, though."

"There will never be another like him. Still, you can't keep putting this off. It's time for you to face this and to give your father's memory rest. I know you wanted to wait for Carmen to wake up to be there with you, but it doesn't look like she's going to wake up soon. Almost everyone else has, but she's... just not responding to any of our medicine. You'll have to do this without her."

Raesh nodded his head and began walking back across the shore. The river flowed quick and dark beside him, almost two hundred feet wide at that point. He greeted the fighters as he passed them and stopped to check on some of the more seriously injured ones. Everyone had calmed and cheered up considerably since the traitor was discovered and executed, though they were still on edge about the future. At least, they felt, the worst was over. Hopefully.

Raesh moved on to where Carmen and a few others were lying, still unconscious. Most everybody had woken up and been seen to properly, but Carmen and two other fighters had yet to respond to anything, although the other two did show signs of waking soon. Lilja and Kent were sitting behind Carmen's head, watching over her as they did day and night whenever Raesh way away. Sarinda had woken not long after Andie left, but after finding out the truth about Lilja she had refused to be seen with her. It had been a bitter scene.

Many of the other fighters, most of them in fact, had forgiven Lilja. They understood that she was truly loyal to the cause and had only done what she did in order to protect her family. They understood that they would have done the same. Kent was still his kind and helpful self and had done everything in his power to help Raesh restore some kind of order to the group. Neither he nor Lilja felt at all angry or vengeful about being locked up. They just wanted to help. Raesh sat down beside Carmen and took her hand.

"You better not be thinking of sleeping too much longer," he said. "I need you here. We all need you in ways you can't imagine. You're the only family I have left. I don't know if Andie and the others are coming back and I don't know what news they'll bring if they do. You have to wake up. You have to help me."

"It's hard seeing friends like this," Kent said. "Sometimes I think I don't want them to wake up, because, when they do, all they'll find is carnage. The ship destroyed. Eighty-seven dead. Well, eighty-eight now. Us stranded in the Hot Salts and the future more uncertain than it's ever been. And to wake up and figure out that the traitor was Yara... and that she's dead..."

"It's horrible," Lilja said, looking down at her hands. "It's horrible and it's all my fault. I should've just said no."

"From what you told me it sounds like the University had already turned Yara before they came for you. None of this is your fault," Raesh said. "Any of us would've done the same to protect our family. All you can do now is your part in getting us back on track. That's how you earn our trust back."

Lilja nodded, but never raised her eyes. Raesh knew she'd still be beating herself up for months to come. Kent rubbed more of the balm on Carmen's forehead that the dragonborn had given them. He seemed to want to say something to Raesh, but couldn't figure out how or if he should say it.

"What is it, Kent?" Raesh asked, not angry, but curious.

"I'm just wondering how she'll take the news. Andie, I mean. About what happened."

"I don't know, but I wish I could be there with her when she finds out. I sent a coded message with the bird, like Saeryn asked. Just enough information so that Andie knows what's going on, but not enough so that if anyone on the other side intercepts it, they won't have one up on us."

Kent nodded. "Smart. Have you heard back yet?"

Raesh shook his head. "The message should be getting there soon. I sent it not long after they left. The night that Oren dealt with Yara's execution. I'd give anything to be there by her side when she reads it. After all, I know how devastating it can be to lose someone you love."

CHAPTER TWENTY-TWO

SHE WAS THINKING OF YARA. YARA. YARA. HER BEST friend who she'd turned on at the first sign of trouble. Her best friend who she'd refused to give the benefit of the doubt and never even given a chance to explain herself, defend herself. Her best friend who had turned on them all and was now likely gone. She remembered that Carmen had introduced them. She remembered that Yara had been so kind and helpful when she'd first arrived at the Academy and Yara had also been the first to figure out that she was truly a dragonborn.

They had been immediate and true friends, and Yara had literally gone to the ends of the earth with her, had fought with her, suffered with her, been afraid with her. They'd been hiding in the tunnels under the University for months and she was beginning to lose her mind, her calm, but it was Yara who had reassured her and Yara who had forced her to maintain her hope. She couldn't believe how she'd treated her friend, her ally, her fellow soldier. And now she was gone. And there was nothing anyone could do about it. She still hardly believed Yara had been the one to turn on them. That she was the traitor.

The last sight of her—the final image that would have to suffice for the rest of time and pain—had been her being carried away in the jaws of a great green dragon. A huge, fire-breathing dragon, more fearsome than Andie had ever seen her. It had been the one she rode with Oren, and she shivered thinking about how vicious she had appeared when she came to collect Yara in her jaws. She had seemed such a gentle creature when they flew together before.

She wondered what fate Yara had met. Had the dragon simply dropped her from a great height, somewhere along its way back to its cavern? Had it tossed her into the path of lightning and let the legendary bolts of the Hot Salts do the work? Or had it swallowed her whole, condemning her to darkness and a slow death? Did it burn her alive with its terrible, unquenchable fire? Or did it simply crush her in its jaws, just break her irreparably and then never give another thought to the deed? Did she really want to know? She kept repeating to herself in her mind that the dragonborn were a peaceful race. Perhaps the dragon hadn't hurt her at all. She clung to that thought as fiercely as she could. Surely, they wouldn't have harmed her without Andie's consent.

Andie opened her eyes. She was lying on her stomach on the floor and she hurt all over. This was the fourth time in recent days that she'd woken up like this, but this time her mind was perfectly clear. She knew the reason she was hurting so badly was because she had been standing so close to the chancellor when he made his final attempt and blew himself up.

She lifted her face and found that her neck hurt tremendously, too. She looked straight ahead and she could see glass on the carpet. The hole she'd made in the window after the blast hit her was huge and there was glass everywhere. She began the slow process of picking herself up and it was excruciating. But she knew she needed to get back to Saeryn and the others. If they were still there. For all she knew, the spell—with all its millions of sacrifices—had worked perfectly and the dragonborn on Brie were no more. She needed to get back up there to see it for herself.

And even if Saeryn and her people were still alive, millions of people were dead. The chancellor's spell had killed everyone in Arvall, and, regardless of how they had hated the dragonborn or wanted them dead, she knew that they deserved better than the fate that had found them in the end. She was frustrated, confused, and angry with herself for not being able to stop him. She had failed.

She had no idea his hatred could run so deep or that he had been hiding such power and such evil. She knew she would never be able to come to terms with the horror that lay outside. And there was still everyone back in the Hot Salts to think of. A part of her wanted to lie back down and stay there forever. It was all too much.

"We thought you were dead."

Andie sprang to her feet, momentarily disregarding her pain, and spun to face the voice. It was a woman. She was dressed in a knee-length gray skirt and a pink blouse that was almost see-through. She had her hair up in a tight bun and she wore glasses with a thin frame. Just a regular woman. And all around her there were other people dressed in regular, office appropriate clothes. The room was full of people and they were all staring at Andie.

"Who are you?" Andie asked, her hands up and ready to defend herself.

"We work here," the woman said cautiously, backing up a few steps. "We were working last night when everything started turning to chaos. First, there were a lot of screams and then there were these terrible crashes. And then we died. All of us. But a few hours ago, we woke up and we've kind of just been too freaked out to go outside. We were going to wake you, but we didn't know if you were hurt or how badly. And, well..."

"Well what?" Andie shouted.

"Well, you weren't exactly... here last night. And we just wondered where you came from. Who you are..."

"My name is Andie," she said, calming down a little. "I was knocked over here by a blast of magic. I was trying to save you all, but I failed. Which is why I don't understand how you're all alive right now."

"It was the dragon Queen," the woman said. "She brought us back."

Andie stared at the woman for a long moment, trying to process what she had just been told. "I don't understand. Saeryn saved you? How? Is she here? Is she alive?"

"She's not here, but I'm pretty sure she's still alive," the woman explained. "It's kind of hard to explain, but it's like we all got this transmission in our brains. A woman's voice. I just remember hearing this soft voice, chanting in my ear, coaxing me back towards life in a language I didn't quite understand."

Andie sunk to the floor to steady herself. Had they actually won? She had no idea Saeryn was capable of such magic. Part of her didn't believe what she was hearing. But, the woman was alive, so she must be speaking the truth.

"The magic was so strange, so unfamiliar." The

woman bent down on the floor near Andie, smiling softly at her as she recounted her memories. "I remember waking up and feeling like my soul was flying, like my mind was on the back of a dragon or something. It was breathtaking and terrifying all at once. But then, when I opened my eyes, I was alive. Your dragons gave back our lives after Chancellor Mharú tried to sacrifice us all for a spell."

"The dragons brought you back?" Andie spoke the words softly, only mildly believing it.

Another woman came to join them, placing her hand on Andie's shoulder. "Not long after we woke, we heard voices from the streets. People are saying the dragon Queen saved us and gave us back our lives because they had been taken away from us in an act of such immense evil."

The two women helped pull Andie to her feet when she didn't respond. They led her to the nearest chair and kindly waited for her to collect her thoughts.

Andie tried to think things through. If the women spoke the truth, and she had no reason to doubt them, it meant the dragonborn were still alive. It also meant that the chancellor was truly dead and that everyone else had died but been brought back. The truth was finally about to be exposed. She was confused at first until it finally dawned on her. It was good news. Something good had finally happened. They'd won.

"Can I have some water?" Andie finally managed to say.

"Sure," the woman said, grabbing a bottle off of her desk. "Are you okay?"

"Yeah, it's just," Andie began. "I don't know. It's over. I'm not sure if I believe it."

The woman who handed her the water smiled. "You look confused."

Andie nodded. "I am. I think… I think I'm happy."

"Is that unusual?"

"For my life? You'd be surprised."

Andie drank the water and rested for a moment while her body began to heal. When she felt stronger she stood, thanked the women, and then led all of them outside where they met a huge crowd of people standing in the street. An excited chatter filled the streets, hundreds of people gathering together and speaking frantically, each looking around and above them, searching for something. Andie walked up to the first person she saw.

"What's going on?" she asked.

"We're waiting for her to come back around again."

"Who?"

"The dragon Queen."

Andie gasped and grabbed the man by his shoulders so abruptly that she startled him. "What do mean 'waiting for her to come back around again?' What is she doing?"

"She's been flying around the city for hours now. She's looking for someone, I think."

Andie let him go and started making her way through the crowd. She pushed through until she made it to the center of the intersection and then she cleared a small circle around herself.

"Everybody stay back!"

She raised her arm straight in the air and sent up a beam of purple light that soared so high it touched the soft, morning clouds. She held it there, burning bright but not hot, the beam itself buzzing slightly as it blasted through the sky. She knew that if Saeryn was still in the city or anywhere within ten miles she would be able to see the beacon. And sure enough, Andie soon heard the powerful sound of pumping wings and as she turned she saw the dragon beating through the sky toward her, Saeryn leaning low on its back.

The crowd backed away, leapt away, and cleared the entire intersection and when the dragon landed it had all the space it could want. Saeryn had jumped from its back even before it hit the ground and at the same instant Andie was rushing toward her. They threw themselves into each other's arms, rejoicing that the other was alive and that there was finally peace.

"You never came back and we had no idea what

had happened to you," Saeryn said, still breathing heavily. "And I came down to find you, but I had no idea where to start. I've searched for you for hours. Are you okay? What happened?"

"I'm fine. I'm so sorry. The chancellor blew himself up as a last measure to ensure that everything died and I got caught in the blast and didn't wake up until just now. But all these people should be dead. You should be gone. What happened?"

"I don't know. This many people dying in sacrifice should have been enough power to fuel the spell a hundred times over. We should have been torn from the earth, but instead the fissure closed. We lived. All I can think is that he performed the spell wrong. Andie, what happened to him? What did you do?"

"Nothing. I took him down, but that was all. I swear. He wasn't wounded in any way that he couldn't have healed from. He just didn't want to accept defeat. He ended it."

Saeryn exhaled a sigh of relief. Andie saw in her face what she had feared and how much she had feared it.

"Don't worry, Saeryn," she said. "I won't deny that I wanted to kill him, to kill everyone in the battalion, but I know it's not in our nature to kill. And I also know that you would never have looked at me the same if I had done something like that."

Saeryn touched Andie's face and they hugged again, now totally free.

Whispers began getting louder around them. Andie couldn't help but smile as she heard people asking their neighbors excitedly if that was the dragon Queen, if she was the one who they heard in their head when they were brought back to life.

"Excuse me," a shy-looking man mumbled softly as he stepped towards Andie and Saeryn. "I'm sorry, but... Are you the dragon Queen? Are you the one who brought us back?"

Andie turned to the man and placed her hand on his shoulder. "She is. This is Saeryn."

The man chewed his lip as he looked to be searching for the right words. He wrung his hands together and then finally knelt down and bowed his head. Others did the same as whispers of thanks began echoing from the buildings around them.

"It was not me," Saeryn spoke to the crowd. "It was not my magic that brought you back. It was the magic of the dragons and of my people, as a whole. It was the magic of good that grew stronger than I had ever seen it grow. A magic that came together to vanquish evil. It is not me you need to thank, but my people and our dragons."

The man looked up with wide-eyes, tears brimming his lids. He then spoke with a quiver to his voice, but he spoke loud so all could hear. "I'm sure I speak for everyone when I say, thank you. Thank you to you all. Thank you for saving us. How can we ever repay the debt?"

Saeryn bowed her head to the man. "We ask no repayment. We did what was right, and we had luck on our side. All I ask is your acceptance of our people. We would like to stay in your city for a time."

Everyone in the crowd grew silent for a moment, and then excited cheers erupted through the crowd as far as Andie could hear. They seemed to really be coming around.

"But what about the University?" someone asked. "The professors and all the people who work for them? What are we gonna do about them? We can't just let 'em go, this would start all over again."

"They'll be taken care of," said Saeryn. "For now, they are no longer a danger to any of you. I understand you're angry and if you decide to execute them, my people and I will not interfere with your laws, but I would urge caution and wisdom. It is compassion that separates us from them and if you sacrifice that then you may as well align yourself with the enemy. I believe you have a very fine prison in this city and I think it would make an excellent permanent home for those who tried to rob you of your freedom and your lives."

There was some hesitation in the crowd. Many of them seemed to really favor execution, but Saeryn's words appeared to be having the desired effect. After some more deliberation, they seemed to agree that it was probably best, but they wanted to hold a formal tribunal soon to be thorough.

"And what about the University itself?" a small, elderly lady asked. "Is it still going to be a military training facility?"

"No," Andie said immediately. She had thought this through long and hard in her months below ground. Her dreams of a new University where all are welcome. "We're done gearing up for war. I think we can do something better with it. We'll build it around new ideas. Truth. Safety. And everyone, absolutely everyone, will be welcome to attend. I know that together we can rebuild this world. The hate for my people has spread far and fast, but we can end that. And we can end hate for everything else, too. I know we don't live in an ideal world and lofty wishes aren't always practical, but there's more to life than this and I think we all know that."

"Will you lead it?" a young boy asked from within the crowd.

"No. But I'd like to attend it," Andie smiled down at him. "I have a friend who'd be perfect for the job, though."

The voices around her grow louder as people began speculating who this person might be. Andie raised her voice and spoke clearly, for all to hear. "His name is Lymir. He is a great and wise man, and we should all be lucky to have him as a leader at the new University. We will, of course, consult the public officially before appointing him, but I can assure you there is no one greater to lead us into our new time of peace."

"Who is this man? What has he done to have earned your trust?" the mother of the boy stepped forward, her arms held firmly on her son's shoulders.

"That is a story for another time," Saeryn answered. "But trust me when I say, Andie is correct. There is no greater person to lead everyone into this new era."

Shouts of Lymir began echoing through the streets as the message passed on. Saeryn turned to Andie.

"What will you do?" the boy called up to Andie.

"I guess I could head up the hortological magic department. Someone's gotta make it right."

There were some laughs among the crowd and Andie herself smiled, though it did make her think of Ashur and where he'd gotten off to. She turned to Saeryn and without a word expressed to her all the gratitude and belief that was piled up inside of her. Without a word, Saeryn returned it.

The two of them were about to mount the dragon and leave when the people they had been talking to kneeled. They were both surprised and were even more so when they saw that many others were following the example. Andie turned to look behind them and saw that everyone was beginning to kneel down. In all four directions, as far as the eye could see, all the people were kneeling low. Andie was humbled and warmed by the sight.

"I think they truly respect you," she said, turning to Saeryn.

"I think so. But make no mistake, Andie... they are paying homage to you, too."

CHAPTER TWENTY-THREE

OVER THE NEXT FEW WEEKS, THE DRAGONBORN remained among the citizens of Arvall City. The people were happy to have them, though there was a transition period when people had to convince themselves not to be afraid and to accept that everything they had been taught over the course of their lives was nothing more than a pack of ugly lies.

Saeryn was elected to a special board that was put in charge of the city until a formal government could be established in the region. The board was responsible for creating new legislature and carrying out a total restructuring of the city's cultural and historical institutions. The civilians made an honest effort to erase everything that disparaged or lied about the dragonborn. And since the dragonborn had been pulled from a past centuries before, they were perfect for helping to rewrite the history books to present the absolute truth.

The professors, Searchers, monitors, battalion soldiers, and even the Sentinels were tried for high crimes against the city, the region, the dragonborn, and all of Noelle. The professors were stripped of their degrees and titles, banned from ever being in positions of power again. The Searchers were forced to hand over all weapons and to provide the special board with any and all knowledge of the kidnappings, disappearances, murders, and memory erasures they had perpetrated over the years.

The result of those interviews was a harrowing collection of volumes listing too many evils to comprehend. The white fire and the deighilt were taken from the hooded monitors, who were also banned from any positions and forced to write detailed confessions. The battalion soldiers ceded their armor to the city. The Sentinels were shut down and hidden away where they couldn't hurt anyone ever again.

The trials took place over the weeks and the information that came out during those days was sickening. All of the people who had been willingly involved in Chancellor Mharú's crimes were sentenced to prison, without any possibility of ever being released. In fact, they were sent to a holding facility until the dragonborn could help the city finish constructing a special prison with defenses that couldn't hope to be outsmarted. Where they were going, there was no hope. Yet many thought they were still getting off easy; after all, if it hadn't been for Saeryn all the conspirators would have been guilty of the murder of an entire city. Approximately six million people. In an odd turn of events, the dragonborn and members of the local police force had to protect the conspirators, lest the civilians have their way with them.

The city had a hard time rebuilding itself. Saeryn and the dragonborn had given them back their lives, but there was still a lot of physical damage to the city. The chancellor's final wave of magic, having been amplified enormously by his armor, had destroyed and completely blown out a number of buildings and he had already begun a widespread demolition of parts of the city in order to expand the new military University. Much had to be reconstructed and much could never hope to be salvaged.

The University also had to be remodeled, stripped of all its propaganda and military aspirations. The chancellor had certainly left his mark on everything he touched and there was no denying that the people had a long way to go before they could rediscover normal.

Chancellor of West Noelle, Myamar Mharú, became a name no one even whispered. His image and likeness was taken off of every wall, tossed out of every building, burned in the middle of the streets in large piles that burned all night and smoked all morning. His many laws and edicts were struck from the books and every office he had in the University or the city was cleaned out, destroyed and redesigned. Everything he'd left his mark or imprint on was destroyed and they performed this action again and again and again, all throughout the University and the city, until every trace of him was removed.

The board decided to keep a special section with files on the chancellor and the horrors he had committed—they never wanted history to repeat itself. The costs would be too high.

A search began for the soldiers that got away. Some of the men Andie had fought on the train were caught and imprisoned, but according to the battalion's register quite a few got away. Some men had escaped during the night, but a large group of others had already been stationed at the edge of the city. By the time the dragonborn got there, the building was empty.

A wider search began throughout the region, but no one had the first idea about where those men had gone. Many feared that Ashur would lead them back and another war would begin. It was made an even greater fear by Saeryn vowing to never again abuse the magic of blood and dragons to tempt fate. If anything like this ever happened again, the city would be in huge trouble.

Yet the hardest chore of all was trying to decide how they would convince the rest of Noelle that the dragonborn were not only not a threat, but were allies. Saeryn was asked to send more telepathic messages, but she declined—she knew that the messages only worked the first time because those people in the city had seen firsthand what kind of man the chancellor was and she had brought them all back to life. Without those particular circumstances, the messages would only be seen as more lies.

They thought it might be a good idea to send ambassadors, a mix of dragonborn and the most respected citizens of Arvall; perhaps a delegation of that composition would be well received, or at least *received* in the first place, and have a fighting chance at changing people's mind. There was also talk of simply inviting people to Arvall to see the dragonborn in-person, get to know the people and see that they were completely kind and did not have wickedness in their nature. Many more plans were also put forth, but so far nothing had been selected as especially promising.

Raesh and the others from the Hot Salts of Mithraldia had not yet arrived, but were hopefully only a few days out. It had taken so long because a sturdy ship had to be found that could survive the Gray Fold. It took that ship four weeks to reach the group where they were and would take even longer to get back. Several messages had been sent with the crew of the ship for the fighters, and news of the dragonborn victory elated them to no end. Instructions were also sent and Lymir began to prepare in earnest for his new position.

Many of the fighters were ecstatic to be going home and to not have to fight, but there were still some concerns. A faction of them decided to go off on foot and look for the remainder of the battalion, taking some supplies from the new ship and saying goodbye to their friends. Kent and Lilja were among those who left. Lilja feared what might happen to her if she ever went back to Arvall; she was not convinced that she would be forgiven or pardoned, even though Raesh gave her his word. Kent went with her to keep her company and keep her strong.

Everyone else who had been seriously injured in the explosion had woken up by the time the ship arrived. Except Carmen. Her condition was stable and her health hadn't deteriorated any further, but something was clearly wrong. Everyone else was awake and for some reason Carmen simply wasn't responding. They were hoping that something could be done for her in Arvall or that Saeryn might be able to help her.

They set sail from the Hot Salts loaded down with provisions from the dragonborn people and a flurry of good wishes. The dragonborn were sad to see them go: the two races had learned a lot from each other in the weeks the fighters were among them.

Since the University was going to be all-inclusive now, Raesh had offered himself as an instructor. He thought he might teach classes for people without the gift of magic—though he himself was a pearlblood, he'd spent most of his life pretending to be human and was probably the most qualified to teach those classes. He wanted to help people, but he also wanted another direction for his life. Fighting and secrets and death had had a hold over him for too long. He wanted to be something his father would have been proud of. He wanted to do something good, something worth remembering.

He also wanted to finally publish his books, something he knew he should have done long ago, but hesitation was behind him now. The only other thing he wanted was Andie. They had been apart so much lately and it was as painful to him as watching his friends die. He needed her in ways he couldn't explain and he only hoped she felt the same way.

There was peace all around.

The only person who wasn't doing well was Andie. Not long after they'd defeated the chancellor and his battalion, a messenger bird arrived from the Hot Salts. It carried a torn tear-streaked letter addressed to Andie written in Raesh's messy scribble.

My cousin has yet to wake up.

The traitor has been executed.
Your father has passed on.

Andie had to reread the message multiple times before she could fully comprehend what the letter was telling her. Her vision swam and her mind worked a league a minute as she processed her thoughts. Carmen was in a coma and Marvo had been executed. Well, not really, she thought, as he had blown himself up in his attack. But her eyes filled with tears as she read that last line over and over. Her father was dead. Her chest felt like it was going to implode. She wasn't sure her body was able to take the news. Grief filled her very core and she began to shake, not wanting to accept the words as true. She had just lost a part of her.

Your father has passed on.

She didn't want to believe it. He had looked to be doing so much better. No, she couldn't believe it. She... Andie then read the line before it and dropped the letter on the floor.

The traitor has been executed.

Andie flustered, trying to recall the events of the past few days. Everything had happened so fast. The attacks, the magic, the death, the new life. She tried so desperately to remember her interactions with Raesh back at the ship, but she quickly realized she hadn't communicated with him or anybody else since discovering the truth.

"Yara," Andie whispered as she fell to her knees.

Marvo was the traitor, not Yara. Marvo was the one who betrayed them all, although not knowingly. It had been he who had been spelled, or so the chancellor had said. Raesh wouldn't have known the truth. But everyone at the ship would still think Yara to be the one who betrayed them. Yara wasn't the traitor. Yara was innocent.

Yara was dead.

For days on end, Andie refused to come out of the room they'd set up for her in the city. She couldn't face herself after what she'd done. Her best friend was killed because Andie was too blinded by anger to bother confirming her suspicions. She had been killed for nothing. Andie couldn't look herself in the mirror, let alone face anybody else. She felt broken. Betrayed by her own actions. She could never forgive herself.

What was worse, is that beyond the anger and grief and self-loathing, she had an irreparable sadness for the loss of her father. A sadness she felt was unfair for her to feel, as how can someone who had done something so terrible be allowed to feel sorry for herself like she was. But still, despite her fierce determination to not allow herself to feel the sorrow that came from a parent's death, she still mourned.

Her father had been seriously injured, and he had given her the signs. She could have done something to prevent him from getting worse, but she didn't. She left. He mentioned something about a headache and dizziness. Now he was dead, too, and it was all because of her.

Carmen was just as tragic a thought. She should never had been in that cell, anyway, and if she hadn't been so close to Marvo, she would still be conscious. Maybe even unharmed. She had taken Andie under her wing at the Academy and had shown her how to have fun and enjoy life. Now she was lying in a coma and there were no signs that she was ever going to wake up.

Andie cursed herself for ever even doubting Carmen, for not believing in her and in the person that she had already proven herself to be. It was far, far less than a true friend and ally deserved. And now Andie was left with nothing but a collection of bitter memories that was made even more painful by how sweet and beautiful they were.

Andie couldn't stand herself. She felt sick, trapped inside the body of someone who had betrayed her friends and family. It was her fault that they were gone. She could never forgive herself for it.

The days passed. And then the weeks. Soon enough a new year had come around and the University was getting very close to its reopening. The rebuilding of the city had come quite a long way, though there was still much work to be done.

Still, the city was alive again. The people were

happy, excited about the future. The dragonborn were still living on Brie, for the time being, and the ship was only a few days out from arriving at the port. Everything seemed to be advancing. Everyone seemed to be moving on.

Everyone, part from Andie.

CHAPTER TWENTY-FOUR

"THIS ISN'T HEALTHY," OREN SAID, PACING BACK AND forth. Since arriving back from spending some time on the ship with their allies he had been trying to speak with Andie, but she hadn't allowed any visitors. He was growing impatient. "I've worried for her before, but never like this. When it came to the University and the chancellor's many plots, she at least immersed herself in the support system around her. She allowed each of us to do our parts and in the end we succeeded. But she's changed. It's as if she thinks she's alone now and she won't speak to anyone. She barely even looks at you, and you're the one person she looks up to."

"It was a victory for us, Oren," Saeryn said softly. "But it was hard-won. The people of Arvall were all dead, she'd failed to save them. We managed to give

293

them back their lives, but at great cost to our strength. Even I didn't think we could have managed such a feat. Our beloved dragons gave them a second chance, despite the hate and evil that they had harbored for us before. But Andie's friends, the fighters who left home and aligned themselves to our cause, they all died. And no one was there to revive them."

"She must surely see the good in what she's done, though?" Oren finally stopped pacing and faced his Queen. "Surely she knows the deaths are not her fault."

"Her own father died," she replied. "Her best friend is lost. Another is still sick. It must be hard on her to understand how all this was fair. She must also be thinking about how awful things would have been if the chancellor won, which he very nearly did. And now she's supposed to teach in the very same building that housed the people who hated her most?"

Oren slumped against the wall. He wore casual linens now, no longer requiring his dragon-scaled armor his people were renowned for. He was growing used to the simple life among the people in their strange, modern time. "I suppose it has been far harder on her than on anyone else."

"She still believes it's her responsibility to save the world. She's only just learning that we can't save everyone, even if we're only trying to protect the ones we love. Even in a war with an outcome as favorable as this there are consequences. I only wish she wasn't the one who had to suffer them. She still believes she failed in regards to her father and her friends."

"Is it her father that has gotten to her the most?"

Saeryn shrugged. "Perhaps. Although she does not seem one to lose herself to grief so strongly. No, I suspect it is her involvement in the loss of her friend that is eating away at her. Yara, the girl we punished for being the traitor."

"I must speak to her about that," Oren said suddenly. "She knows not the truth of what happened."

Saeryn considered. "Perhaps that is wise. But not just this moment. We have things we need to attend to."

Saeryn and Oren turned and headed back into the University to finish overseeing the new design. Saeryn was met almost immediately by one of the other members of the board. He name was Stefan. He had been invited to Arvall City from Taline to the north. Now that the chancellor's personal files had been opened and reviewed, it had been revealed that the University was responsible for every terrorist attack in Taline for the last twenty years. Chancellor Mharú's unbelievable crimes had nearly destroyed the city that Stefan had worked so hard to protect. The other board members thought it only right that Stefan should be invited to the city to help define its new direction. He and Saeryn had become fast friends.

"It's a relief to know that something good is finally going to come from this place," he said. "I've spent so many years wondering if or how Myamar was responsible for the tragedies that have plagued my city. Now I know."

"That one man did a great deal of evil against us all," Saeryn replied. "But he's gone now."

"And for that I'm grateful. I understand that Andie Rogers is the girl I should thank for finally setting the world back on course."

"Indeed, she is."

"I was once on the council of Taline with her father. He was a good man. I was sorry to hear that he passed. I'm afraid I was once as nearsighted as the rest of the region. I regret it, but I had been taught that the dragonborn were evil, not to be trusted. I nearly harmed him and his wife once. You can imagine my shock and sadness when I learned later that she had been taken that very same night."

"The fact that you are here now tells me everything I need to know about you. My people and I are not in the habit of holding onto past grudges."

"That helps me a great deal to know. But I wonder about Andie. I can't imagine what stories her father told her about me. I was never very open with him, but it was only because I took our sworn duty so seriously. I always thought very highly of him. And I never forgot the face of his wife, that beautiful woman who was so atrociously mistreated. I never met Andie. I'd like to meet her now. Soon, if she'd be up for it."

"I'm sure she will in time," Saeryn said with a heavy sigh. "But right now, she is coming to terms with the terrible weight of her losses. Many lives and many dreams had to be sacrificed for this victory, and no one has had to bear the brunt of that pain more than Andie. But I will make sure she knows your intentions."

Stefan gave Saeryn a terrifically honorable bow and then disappeared down another hallway. Saeryn continued forward, lending her expertise wherever it was needed and stopping every so often just to encourage and reassure people. It was hard work and had taken a lot of effort, and would require still more later.

Saeryn had offered any number of times to assist them, to help in any way she could, but the citizens thought her position as Queen was too majestic for menial chores. She tried explaining to them that among the dragonborn not even the Queen is above contributions and that she was no stranger to hard work, but they wouldn't listen. They were just trying to pay her back in the only way they knew they could. And so, she fulfilled the role they crafted for her and made sure she was always around to boost morale.

The dragonborn and the citizens were learning so much from coexisting, from leaving behind hate and moving forward in peace. The new spirit of cooperation would be reflected in all of the new paintings, decorations, and especially in the course selection for the new classes. Some dragonborn had even been asked to remain in Arvall City and teach classes at the University, while some of the scholars and researchers from Arvall had been invited to the Hot Salts to live among the dragonborn and learn more.

Saeryn continued down into the very bowels of the University, where the corridors were. They were still in the process of removing the University's heartless celebration of all the death and pain it had caused. Instead, the walls would be covered in an iridescent mural telling the history and struggle of the dragonborn people. The mural had already begun in some parts and when it was finished would be leagues long. She stayed to watch some of the painting and then left, on to supervise other tasks and lift other spirits.

Saeryn was happy. She knew she was happy and she knew that the only thing that could make it better was to see Andie happy. Her people were finally safe, finally accepted, and she wanted Andie to share in that more than anyone, because it was Andie who had lived alone all those years, without her mother, without her people, and it was time she knew the life she should have had all along. When she was done in the University, Saeryn boarded SKY 6—which had been rebuilt for a second time and hopefully the last—and rode down Brie.

Traveling on the dragon was faster, and, like all dragonborn, Saeryn loved the open air and the sun on her skin, but she was also in awe of the modern technology. When she reached the bottom, she walked directly over to the place where Andie was staying—the place she hardly ever came out of. Saeryn walked right up to the door and rather than knock, she simply spoke.

"Andie, it's me. May I come in?"

"Why not?"

It was as melancholy an answer as she had ever heard, but perfectly in line with what Andie had become. Saeryn opened the door to the building and was immediately met with the smell of soldering ash. She quickly looked around to make sure nothing was burning, but when she saw Andie sitting calmly in the middle of the floor she calmed some. She walked further inside and looked around. The room was filled with books, almost the entire floor was covered with them.

Andie had no furniture, no appliances, just books in every direction. There were piles on the stairs and piles in the kitchen. Andie herself was surrounded by small piles and individual books laid out with their insides exposed. The books looked ancient, so old in fact that some were showing warnings that they were preparing to fall apart. Saeryn's first instinct was to ask what Andie was doing, but she could well imagine what kind of answer that would get her. Instead, she sat down beside Andie and said nothing.

"To what new catastrophe do I owe this visit?" Andie asked, never looking up from her book. "Another one of my friends die?"

Saeryn didn't say anything. She merely kept sitting and looking around her.

"Look, if you're here for another heart-to-heart I appreciate it, but it's not what I need right now."

Still nothing. Andie began to get annoyed.

"I know you only want the best for me, and I know that seeing me in pain isn't easy for you, but please... Saeryn, you're really freaking me out just sitting there looking around like that."

"You have my blood."

Finally, Andie looked up. She thought she'd misheard Saeryn or maybe misunderstood what she meant.

"What?" she asked. "What did you say?"

"You have my blood."

"What do you mean?"

"It is common knowledge about our heritage among the dragonborn, but perhaps that knowledge got wiped away as the years passed and the sorcerers destroyed our books and our histories in your world. It is the coloring that gives it away."

"Coloring? What do you mean?" She was curious but also disinterested. She ran her fingers along the floor as she listened, partially lost in her own thoughts.

Saeryn reached out and stroked Andie's unkempt amethyst hair. "Each family shares a coloring, Andryne."

Andie's attention snapped back up at the sound of her full name. She considered what Saeryn was saying and realization slowly dawned on her. She gazed forward at Saeryn's beautiful, silken magenta hair. "We share the same coloring."

Saeryn nodded and smiled. "Not only that, but a dragon does not just let anyone ride it. There are only two instances a dragon allows a rider on its back who is not its rightful pair. The first, is if you are family, related to the rider."

Andie considered a moment and nodded. "That explains why I rode your dragon, I suppose. What about Oren's?" The mere thought of Oren's name send a shiver up her spine. She tried to push the thought of him and his dragon away, but all she could see now was the memory of his beast taking Yara away.

Saeryn tilted Andie's chin up so they locked eyes. "The second, is if that rider is of royal blood. A dragon will allow the royal lineage to ride its back, regardless of who their true rider is. I'll admit I don't fully understand it, but it dates back to the earliest days when the dragons first roamed the earth and we first bonded with the magnificent creatures. I believe our family, the royal line, were the first to bond with the dragons."

Andie stared wide-eyed at Saeryn, her thoughts working wildly as she tried to grasp what she was hearing. "But I don't understand. How can that be?"

"I believe we are from the same lineage."

"I… What? But you're from over one thousand years before. What does this even mean?"

"It means, my sweet Andryne. That you are born to be the dragonborn Queen. You are my heir."

Andie swallowed hard and shook her head. "Impossible. I'm no Queen. I'm a murderer… I couldn't even save my friends. I have no right to any throne."

"Andie, you are my blood. Whether you chose to accept this or not, you are a dragonborn ruler. One day you will be the Queen of the dragonborn."

Andie was dumbfounded and she almost fell over from the shock. She wasn't exactly happy or sad or angry or anything. With all the joy she felt at having beaten the University and the pain she felt at having lost so much and so many, she hadn't really known how she felt in weeks. She was completely convoluted inside. And now Saeryn was telling her that she was royalty and would be Queen someday. Queen. She wondered if it was good news, if it was bad news, or if it was just one more thing she had to consider her duty to fulfill.

"Andie, the first thing you need to understand is how happy I am to know that you are my blood and how proud I am of everything that you have done, every trial and hardship that you have battled through to be here today. You are so strong it makes my heart burst to look at you. But the time for your self-pity is at an end. I have allowed you to grieve as much as I felt necessary, but now you must hold fast and gather your courage. There is a long road ahead and millions of people in this city and in this region will be looking for someone to lead them, someone to make them believe again. The dragonborn want someone to be a link between their world and this new one that we find ourselves flung into. I want with all my soul for that person to be you.

"I know what you've lost and I know that it hurts unlike any other pain you're ever likely to feel again, but what is done cannot be undone. We have all suffered a great deal. The other dragonborn suffered these same losses centuries ago when the war against us first began. Yet here we stand. You are royalty. And, far more than simply a silly title, being royalty means leading, inspiring, and protecting. You cannot allow yourself to be this person that you've become. You mean too much to too many people. I need you too much to watch you whither like this."

Saeryn touched Andie's face and wiped the tears that had begun to fall. Andie was hurting so deeply inside that there didn't seem an end to the pain, but she knew Saeryn was right. She had known it for quite some time now. She recognized that none of her pain would ever fully be healed, but there would come a point when she would have to focus, to pick herself up and go on with the business of living. That point had come. If the dragonborn needed her, if Arvall City needed her, she would be there.

"Of course," Andie said. "Back in the Hot Salts, Oren looked shocked when his dragon let me ride her. It all makes sense now. But I still don't think I…"

"You are the strongest person I've met. Not only that, but you are unique. You represent everything this world needs right now. You are sorcerer and you are dragonborn. There is no one better to represent our people in this new era of peace."

The words were too much for her to handle, but Andie knew it was her duty to stay strong. To stay true to herself, and part of her always knew there was more to this life than what she had grown up believing. Finally, she nodded. Accepting her fate as best she could, given the circumstances.

"So, what happens now? Do the rest of our people know that I'm your heir?"

"Well, I haven't made a formal pronouncement, but I'm sure once they saw you riding my dragon they figured it out. I can assure you, this news will please them all. I don't know if you yet understand how much the people love you. You've done more for them than you know."

"I'm just glad to have them."

"Good. Now that we've come to an understanding, there are things we should talk about. But first, Oren wants to speak with you."

Anger flashed across Andie's face at the mention of his name. "No, I will not see him."

"Andie, he has information you need to know. Information that I think will lighten your heart and help you move on from the darkness that has bound you to this room for all these months. You must hear him." Saeryn placed her hand on Andie's cheek as she spoke, and when Andie didn't respond, she turned to leave the room and Oren stepped through the door in her place.

"Say whatever it is you have to say and then leave," Andie said coolly. "I have nothing I want to say to you."

Oren narrowed his brow as he looked down at Andie on the floor, but he quickly closed door and joined her in the center of the room. It took him a long while to collect his thoughts, but when he finally spoke, his voice held warmth and compassion.

"Andie, about Yara," he began.

Andie's heart beat wildly in her chest as she listened. Her best friend, Yara. Mistaken for a traitor and wrongfully executed at the hands of the man before her. She hated him almost as much as she hated herself. "Speak."

"It is not the dragonborn way to kill. It was my duty to deal with the traitor, but when the time came, I was unable to see it through."

Andie sat up straighter, frozen in place. What had he just said?

Oren continued, "I sent her through a time spell. I couldn't be responsible for killing one of our own, so I sent her through a portal, back towards where I once came."

Andie's mouth hung open. "You didn't kill her." She could hardly believe her ears. She pushed herself up off the floor and began to pace the room, repeating the words to herself. She turned to Oren abruptly and froze again in place. "So, she's alive?"

Oren nodded solemnly and held his hand on Andie's shoulder. "She is. Just not in our time. Andie, Yara is gone. It is best not to dwell on it, but I hope that knowing she was not killed brings you some peace."

Andie's eyes filled with tears as she flung her

arms around the man before her. He stood there, awkward for a moment, but then wrapped his arms around her and held her close as she wept. The two stood there in their embrace for many long minutes until Andie finally regained her breath and wiped away the tears.

"Thank you, Oren." She unwound herself from his arms and stepped back from him, letting out a deep breath she had been holding. "Thank you."

Oren nodded and turned to leave. He turned back to look at her as he held the door open. "You will make a great ruler, Andie. I am honored to serve you." And with that, he walked out of her room and Andie listened to his footsteps as they disappeared into the silence.

A moment later, Saeryn rejoined Andie in her room. Andie beamed at the Queen, the weight of guilt finally lifted from her heart. But her smile was short-lived as she recognized the pain in Saeryn's eyes.

Saeryn took a deep breath and looked down at her hands for a moment. It was a thing she rarely did, a gesture of hesitation. Generally, she was a woman of action and conviction. If there was something she was having trouble saying to Andie, it couldn't be good.

"As you know, we've sent out warriors to track down the rest of the battalion, but so far we haven't had any luck. However, this morning those warriors came back with news of a different problem. As they were flying back over the String Fields to reenter the city, there was a message burned in the fields."

"What did it say?"

"*Fhealltóir Fola*. It means blood traitor and it is from a language that is no longer spoken in your era. I think convincing the rest of Noelle is going to be a much larger issue than we initially believed. Before the University attacked us, there were others who either envied us or sought our power. And none of them was so darkly vicious as a certain group from the north. They haunted us and tormented us in ways the University couldn't even dream of. When the University finally did begin to come after us, this group disappeared. We assumed they'd moved out of Noelle or died off. But this message was their calling card once upon a time and it is a phrase only they or a dragonborn would know."

"Do you think they've been hiding all these years?"

"Why not? The world assumed we were dead and yet here we are. Why should they be any different? Andie, if these people are still alive, then there are no doubts about it. There will be war. And much of it."

"That's the last thing we need. They've got to be close. The String Fields border Arvall on the eastern side. That's just outside of the city."

"And make no mistake. They will come."

Andie looked around her at her books. She looked back up at Saeryn with a devilish grin.

"Then let them come."

"What?" Saeryn said, shocked. "Andie, I don't think you understand."

"Look to your right. Pick up one of those thin volumes in the far pile."

Saeryn turned and reached for the book. She brought it into her lap and began to study it. It wasn't until she opened the cover that she gasped.

"This is a journal from the House Erato, one of the seven founding families of Arvall!" she said, turning it over in her hands and observing every inch of it. "This is incredible. Where did you find such a thing?"

"In Leabharlann. Now that we have unrestricted access, I'm finding all kinds of things you wouldn't believe. I have journals from all seven of the founding families and I've been studying them. You won't believe the secrets they were keeping, even from each other. Even within the families there was strife. But what's most interesting is that of all the visits they made to study the past and to visit different places in their contemporary time, they only made one journey to the future. And you can't imagine what they found."

"What?"

"That's a long story. But look around you again and this time look closely."

Saeryn began to look at the books again, everyone within reach. She peered closer and began to read the names and the dates. As she did so, she began to move faster and faster getting more and more excited and falling further and further into disbelief. Her heart was racing and Andie could hear her breath changing. Finally, Saeryn looked back at Andie.

"They're grimoires! Our grimoires!"

"These were stolen from the dragonborn and they date back almost a thousand years," Andie said. "And the University wasn't just stealing from us. They stole from dozens of different tribes and cities. There's more knowledge and power here than any one group of people could ever amass on their own. It's part of why the University became so powerful and they could've been totally unstoppable, but they could never utilize anything from the ones they stole from us. Only someone with dragonblood could use these spells. And more still, there are hundreds, thousands of books in the archives that can tell us everything we need to know to rebuild, to unite, to be as we never were before."

"Andie, why haven't you told anyone about any of this?" Saeryn asked, still pouring over the books. "There's so much knowledge and wisdom here. So much beautiful information."

"I was afraid, at first. Knowledge corrupts, warps.

But with your help I can control this. Saeryn, we need specific things to move forward with this."

"Like what?"

"First we'll need professor Marcus Iceubes. He once taught folklore at the University, and he's one of the good guys. Then we'll need salt paint—it's going to help us a long way in our preparations. And finally, I need you to tell me everything you remember about the Old World. We have a lot of work cut out for us, but with the chancellor dead and his weapon destroyed, we have every chance at rebuilding this world into what it was always meant to be."

"And what is that?"

"A place where all races can live together in peace. And a place where dragons can once again fly free in the sky."

EPILOGUE

"I think he's dead."

"He's not dead, he's just unconscious. No one is stronger than he is."

"He's dead, look at him. His heart isn't even beating."

"Shut up. We will save him. We just have to get north."

"This is ridiculous. Why are we slowing ourselves down dragging a dead body?"

"I told you, he's not dead. We just need to get there as soon as we can."

"Even if you're right, he's as good as dead. He's been gone for weeks. All I'm trying to say is that we're wasting valuable and limited resources on him and we don't even fully understand what they can even do for him if we get there."

"What they're going to do is save him. They'll put him back together, and between their magic and the power of his suit, we'll save our greatest weapon. He's our leader. And if there's even the slightest chance that we can save him then it's a chance worth taking. And we can always scavenge or take more supplies when we need them."

"He wouldn't want us to be this careless. We're supposed to move every night, but we can't do that and drag him around with us at the same time. So, we move every three nights and that puts the entire group in danger. They've got dragonborn, Council fighters, and who knows who else out looking for us. You really want to try to save a guy who could die from too much motion?"

"If you're so sure he's dead, then why don't you just dump his body and be done with it? But if you're wrong and he does wake up, and he finds out you tried to ditch him, do you think I'm going to stick up for you?"

The other man shut his mouth and looked around himself peevishly. The entire battalion was watching.

"Now, I think you'll agree that it's best to give him a chance. Even if his body is broken and his breath has left him, we saw what their strange magic did to the people of Noelle. It's not impossible to bring someone back from the dead. We need to get him up north where the forces are, or else we have no hope of defeating them and taking back the world. We're done talking about this. Everybody listen up. Get your gear together and let's get on with it. We have a long journey ahead of us if we're going to make it north and have any hope of defeating these damn barbarians and their dragons. I need three guys to help me carry the bed."

"This is ridiculous. I can't believe we're risking our lives dragging his dead body with us."

"He's not dead, I tell ya. Even if his body is, we'll bring him back. We have to. Without him—without our greatest weapon—we have no chance at destroying those beasts once and for all. We have to try."

"I still think we're wasting our time. That suit can only do so much, and his body is barely in one piece. He's gone. We've lost. It's done. The bloody dragonborn have won."

"Shut up and lift the damn bed. Alright everybody, move."

As the group moved onward in the darkness, the form lay wrapped tightly in bandages, his suit barely clinging to what was left of his body. The battalion marched in silence, the echo of their footsteps the only sound in the dark night. On and on they marched, barely stopping to regain their breath and fill their water canisters.

Throughout the entire night, the men pressed on,

determined to get their one final weapon to safety. They would bring Ashur's destroyed body to their allies in the north. Their hopes had faded, but not necessarily lost. If they could only make it in time to have him brought back, they had a chance. If anything, they could salvage the suit and create a new weapon, perhaps, although most had already given up that hope.

But as they marched, a shadow stirred. Under the tightly-wrapped linens, the power from the suit reached Ashur's very core. His heart began to beat again, and the silence of the night was pierced with his scream.

Their weapon was alive.

Printed in Great Britain
by Amazon

58898401R00192